The
Wo
Chri... ...nce

# The Secret of the Wonderful, Little Christmas Mice

## A Heart Warming Adventure

## Andrea M

authorHOUSE®

*AuthorHouse™*
*1663 Liberty Drive*
*Bloomington, IN 47403*
*www.authorhouse.com*
*Phone: 1-800-839-8640*

*Published by AuthorHouse    06/25/2013*

*ISBN: 978-1-4817-6532-9 (sc)*
*ISBN: 978-1-4817-6531-2 (e)*

*Library of Congress Control Number: 2013910990*

# Contents

# Chapter One
## The Halloween Scheme

This is the story of four, very different, villages that lay at the bottom of Mount Tetrad on the Lighthouse Island. The year was 1935.

The names of these villages were rather self explanatory, Richville, the upper class, fancy homes and fussy people.

Midville, the middle class, wanna be upper-class; some of the homes in Midville were as nice as some of the homes in Richville and some of the people in Midville were very much stressed, trying to keep up.

And then there was Pleasantville nicknamed by some of the upper-classes as 'Peasantville.' The homes in Pleasantville were nice enough but more cottage like, nothing fancy, certainly didn't measure up to Richville standards.

Pleasantville was mainly a fishing village and it's main income came from providing fish to the other two villages, who thought fishing was for the poor and uneducated, those who didn't have the skills to earn a better living. Actually they did fairly well, as fishing for three villages was a productive source of income. During some seasons their income was even better than some of those in Midville but they were, for the main part, a pleasant people who preferred a more pleasant way of life and would never dream of leaving Pleasantville, which is just where our story happens to begin.

Oh yes I did say there were four villages didn't I. Well I'm afraid the fourth one is some what of a mystery. Some say a legend, some say it never existed but the name of the mountain itself denotes that there are, or were, four villages and Miss Jenna Hopkins, an eighth grade teacher for

Pleasantville Junior High, thought this mysterious village would make a good topic for an imaginative writing essay.

'An essay!!!??' Tyler cried from the back of the room, 'but its Halloween,' Tyler was Jenna's thirteen year old brother.
'You'll have two weeks to complete it', replied Miss Hopkins.
'But no one knows anything about this village', declared Matt McGregor, the Mayor's son who was also Tyler's best friend.
A couple of the smart girls in the front row started giggling and one of them, Mildred Hamilton turned to face him. 'That's why it's called *imaginative* she said smirking, it's suppose to come from your imagination". She then proceeded to spell out *i, m, a, g, i, n, a, t, i, o, n,* She was the top speller of her class and quite proud of it. Her friends giggled even more and Miss Jenna Hopkins could see that Tyler and Matt were about to start something.
'Alright girls, that will do, let's start with what we do know', said Miss Hopkins. 'We'll list the facts on the board,' she said as she picked up a book from her desk and started turning the pages. 'Let's see now, oh yes here it is.' 'I'm afraid there's not much to go on but it may give you a few ideas for your essay.' 'Now who would like to come up and read this for me'?
Of course Mildred's hand shot right up, as it usually did for any excuse to show off in front of the class. Miss Hopkins was well aware of this and really didn't want to pick her because she wanted to keep peace with the boys so she quickly chose the only other hand that came up, Billy's but in after thought she regretted it because Billy Becket was a slow reader, and that would only give the girls more excuse to giggle.
'Quiet now' she said as he began.
'*A f-forest now exits*'.

'Exists,' corrected Miss Hopkins as the girls, giggled. 'Shush,' she whispered, continue please.'

*'Where—the—vill-age—once—stood'.*

'Thank you very much said Miss Hopkins, who decided to read the last two sentences herself, as the girls, had started giggling again. She was surprised the boys didn't say anything but Tyler and Matt had other plans for Mildred and her friends.

'The inhabitants were said to be small but had great riches,' she continued, 'till the village was destroyed by an avalanche.'

'My dad says that treasure hunters have been through there but found nothing,' stated Gwyneth Parker, one of Mildred's friends.

Matthew smirked, 'right, treasure hunters, it probably doesn't even exist.'

'Actually there have been a few treasure hunters, said Miss Hopkins, 'some were lost and never heard of again. And what is the name of our mountain' she asked?

'TETRA' yelled Billy proudly, but of course everyone knew that, which only made the girls giggle more.

'That's right, Miss Hopkins went on, and the word tetra means, four of something' she decided that she would give the definition herself instead of asking for it because she knew that only Mildred might possibly know the answer and Jenna couldn't bear to listen to her boast about herself one more time.

'Maybe it means four lighthouses' said Gwyneth.

'Good try, answered Miss Hopkins, but no, (the boys started to giggle so she quickly went on) Tetra is an ancient name, and the mountain was named long before there were lighthouses.'

'The village is said to have treasures brighter than anything ever seen before.' 'Wow' exclaimed some of the students in unison. Well it makes for good story telling anyway and I expect to have some good stories to read.

The bell rang and the kids all ran for the door anxious to get ready for trick or treating.

Tyler rushed into the bakery where he lived with his sister Jenna and his Aunt Millie. He grabbed a few snacks then raced upstairs and threw some things into a bag and ran down stairs as Jenna was coming in. 'Where are you off to in such a hurry,' she asked? 'Jakes' he yelled back as he ran off.

Jake Anderson was a handsome young man who owned 'The Tool Barn' across the street, it was his own tool store and home built in the shape of a barn.

He also just happened to be the best carpenter of all the three villages; well Richville didn't have any carpenters, another job for the poor. But Jake was quite successful, so successful in fact that he could nearly afford to live in Richville, he had certainly come a long way in his young life, but he preferred the quieter and friendlier atmosphere of Pleasantville. Jake was well liked. He was always ready to help anyone, even if it was just assisting a couple of young boys build a Halloween prank.

Jake felt he had a lot to make up for. Although his misfortune was never his fault, there were still some who frowned upon him after all these years, but more about that later.

'Hmm' said Jenna as she watched her brother run off, I think that was one of my good sheets I just saw running out the door, he's up to something.'

'Oh let them have their fun' said Millie, it's Halloween, and we can have fun too at the Halloween dance, I hear Jakes going. Why don't you ask him to go with you?'

Jenna rolled her eyes 'I can't go' she said, I'll be busy handing out treats and getting tomorrows rolls ready' she tied on an apron.

'Tomorrows pan rolls are all ready done my dear' said Millie, 'and you know the dance only starts at ten, well after the children are gone home' she added.

'He probably already has a date' said Jenna.

Not yet said Millie', I saw him at lunch time and asked him, I told him you didn't have a date either'.

'OH, Jenna gasped, 'what did you do that for?'

'Because said Millie, 'I know he likes you, he's just a bit shy that's all, why do you think he comes in here every day.

'He's hungry?' Jenna responded, 'and he can't resist your pies.'

'With Cookies Diner right next door to him' asked Millie?

'But no one beat your pies, said Jenna, besides he's probably not going.'

'He is' said Millie, 'he's on the decorating committee, the mayor had him build a spook ally at the hall, I hear it's really scary.'

As Jenna and Millie got their supper Tyler was busy in the back shop with Jake working on his plan to scare the girls. Jake knew it was all in fun but he didn't know how much Tyler hated those girls or how devious he could be. Matt came over as planned and he brought someone with him.

'I didn't think you'd mind if Billy came along, he said, 'I thought he deserved a chance to get back at those girls too.'

Tyler looked up at Billy chomping on a chicken leg; he almost always had something in his mouth. Tyler remembered how cruel the girls were to him today and also felt that Billy deserved this chance.

'Sure, here you go,' he said, as he passed them some tools. A half hour later they were finished. They had built an eight foot tall monster and set it on a wagon. There was room for one boy to fit under its long robes.

'Wow' said Billy, 'that looks scary'.

'Yea' said Tyler, 'now if we could just make it sound scary'.

Just then Billy let out a long loud disgustingly gross burp. Matt Tyler and Jake just looked at each other.

'Oh, scuse me' said Billy, noticing the startled look on every ones face.

'Amazing,' said Matt 'can you do that again'?

'Fraid so, appens all the time when I eat chicken he replied'.

'Never heard anything quite like that' said Jake, 'that's better than all the sounds in the spook ally'.

'You like that???' asked Billy in surprise. 'It always makes my Mom mad and makes my sisters scream.' The guys laughed.

'It's perfect then' said Tyler.

'It is' asked Billy bewildered?

'Yea' said Matt, no one could make a sound like that and if it makes your sisters scream it'll work on Mildred and her gang too.

'Yea Billy because of your great . . . ah, gift were going to give you the honour of driving the monster wagon' said Tyler.

'You are, said Billy? He had never felt so important in all his life and Tyler and Matt were feeling pretty good about the whole idea as well.


Back at the bakery Millie had talked Jenna into going to the costume dance and while Jenna was tidying up in the kitchen Millie entered wearing a beautiful fluffy white dress and carrying a star shaped wand, 'How do I look,' she asked?

'Wow' said Jenna, 'but who are you'?

'Your fairy god mother' of course Millie answered. 'I was thinking you could go as Cinderella'.

'Well I've got the rags for it' said Jenna.

'Nonsense' said Millie, 'Cinderella didn't go to the ball in rags; I thought this might be more suitable,' she held up a beautiful dress.

'Very nice' said Jenna 'but where did you get it'.

'It was your mothers' Millie replied, 'well she asked me to make it for the Christmas ball that year but she never got . . . to wear it. I think she would like to see you in it.

Just then the door bell rang. Goblins I expect said Millie you go on and change and I'll handle the little goblins. As Millie finished at the door she turned to see Jenna walking down the stairs. O my heavens Jenna you look like a princess.

'I don't know about this' said Jenna.

'Well I do' said Millie grabbing their coats, 'come on lets go'. Jenna didn't want to disappoint Millie who obviously went through a lot of trouble for this but this princess idea, well just wasn't her. She felt uneasy as they walked to the town hall, just up the street and was grateful that most of the ghosts and witches were finished for the night. She thought, with everyone in costume at the dance no one would notice her.

As they walked, Jenna happened to look down a side street and she thought she caught a glimpse of a large goblin flying by but gave her head a shake and walked on. What she actually saw of course was Tyler and Matt's giant monster, and it was chasing Mildred and her friends who were running for their lives, and the louder the monster burped, the louder the girls screamed. When they reached the corner Mildred decided to cross the street to the left and continue running that way but she was in such a panic that she didn't think to tell the girls. They bumped into each other and dropped their candy but just kept on running. Tyler and Matt who were hiding in the bushes ran out to grab the candy; the girls were almost out of sight.

'You can slow down now' yelled Tyler to Billy as he zoomed by.

'Use the break' yelled Matt. But Billy just sped on and a stick landed on the ground by Matt. 'What's that' yelled Tyler?

'The break!!!' cried Matt with a look of panic.

Tyler looked horrified and they both took off running after Billy, who was heading straight into a fence but just before the fence there was a large hole in the ground and the front wheels got caught in it and flipped Billy over the fence into a hay pile.

'BILLY!!!' Matt and Tyler finally caught up. Then suddenly they heard a large belch.

'I think he's ok' yelled Tyler as they frantically pulled the straw off of him.

'Billy, are you ok,' asked Matt as they pulled Billy to his feet?

'Wow' said Billy 'that was fun.'

'You sure made them girls run' said Tyler.

'Yea' whooped Matt 'and look at the candy they dropped.'

'Candy' cried Billy with a gleam in his eye.

'Yea' said Tyler, 'you can have it.'

'Have it all added Matt.' Tyler and Matt were so grateful that Billy was ok they were happy to give him all the candy. They put their wagon monster back together as best they could and headed for the party at the town hall.

The town hall was festively decorated with pumpkins, large bats hanging from the ceiling, witches and goblins. Millie and Jenna were at the refreshment table sipping punch when Mayer McGregor took the stand.

'Welcome, everyone to our spooktacular Halloween party.'

'I'd like to thank everyone for their work in pulling this

together, I'd like to especially thank Jake who donated much of his time and materials to create the spook ally,' he said in a mock scary voice. 'Jake, if you would do the honours and get the festivities started.'

Jake hit a switch which caused spooky music to play as ghosts witches and bats flew across the ceiling. Everyone thought it was spectacular and cheered in delight.

'Well' said Millie, 'it looks like Jake's really out done himself this time.'

'Yea, really,' said Jenna, with a disappointed tone. Millie looked at Jenna, who was looking at Jake, only to see that Jake had a girl on each arm.

'I thought he didn't have a date,' said Jenna. Millie was surprised too and shrugged her shoulders not knowing what to say. Tyler Matt and Billy arrived and joined them at the refreshment table.

'Food' said Billy stuffing his face.

'Hello boys' said Millie, 'are you having a good time?'

'Are you staying out of trouble' asked Jenna? Tyler decided to follow Billy's example and stuff his face, rather than answer Jenna.

Jake made it over to the refreshment table without his escorts, Gertrude and Henrietta, daughters of Mayor Edwards from Richville. They had caught a glimpse of him one day as he was helping the Mayor with some renovations.

Their costumes were extravagant and looked a little out of place among the many homemade costumes in the hall. They were both dressed as princesses in beautiful expensive ball gowns and anxiously awaiting Jakes return as he left with a promise to bring punch. They watched longingly for their prince as he walked away from them. They were really a bit too much for him, quite a bit too much, but he was too kind to tell them so. He really didn't know what to do with them.

'Hey Jake,' said Tyler excitedly.

'Hello boys' replied Jake 'how's it going, staying out of trouble?'

'You sound like my sister,' said Tyler. Jake smiled and looked to Millie and Jenna, 'nice costumes' he said.

'Oh thank you' replied Millie, 'I'm Jenna's fairy god mother; she's Cinderella.'

Just then a high pitched laugh came from behind them. 'CINDERELLA????!!!!!?'

It was Gertrude, with an accent on the rude because she often was quite rude.

'Didn't you know that your not suppose to wear your rags to the ball, Cinderella?'

Actually Jenna's dress did pale in comparison to Gertrude's and Henrietta's.

'Or perhaps your wand just needs a little adjusting Fairy God Mother, wouldn't you say Henrietta?' Henrietta laughed and snickered loudly, behind her.

'So what are you then' said Tyler sarcastically, 'the two ugly step sisters?' Jenna knew that she should stop her brother but she remained silent.

'I think they look the part don't you Billy,' he said, sticking his nose up in the air mimicking Gertrude.

Billy had a mouth full of chocolate cake but found Tyler so amusing that he busted out laughing and the cake went all over Henrietta. 'Oh, my dress' she screamed. It was so funny that even Millie laughed.

Gertrude looked furious. 'Are you ready with our drinks Jake,' she demanded! Everyone looked to Jake, who just wanted to disappear at that moment. He quickly poured the drinks and brought them to their table. Henrietta and Gertrude followed as Jake hoped they would then he quickly made an excuse to check on the spook ally and left them.

'I don't know why the snob sisters don't just stay in snobville' said Tyler.

Matt picked up Millie's wand that was lying on the table and made like he was trying to make the snob sisters vanish.

'Blast, he said, they won't disappear.'

'Maybe it does need a little adjusting said Millie' laughing.

'I know what needs adjusting' said Tyler and he motioned for the boys to follow him.

'Stay out of trouble said Jenna', as they walked off.

'Can I have your attention' Mayor McGregor called out, 'it's time to judge the pies and we do have some very delicious looking pies here'. 'Now because one of them was made by my sweet wife Flossie I have decided to turn the job of judging over to Jake who certainly deserves a treat especially after all the work he's done here.' Every one cheered for Jake. 'But to make it completely fair', he continued, 'Jake will not know who the pies belong to, so, Jake if you will'? Jake came up and stood at the pie table where there were twelve pieces of pie waiting for him. Jake didn't really like being put on the spot like this but he didn't know how to say no and thought the sooner he started the sooner he could get it done.

They were all pumpkin pies. He tasted the first; he wondered if it was Millie's, he would really like to pick hers as the winner.

'Good luck Millie,' said Jenna.

Millie smiled, 'thank you dear.'

Jake finished tasting each pie and pointed out to Mayor McGregor the three pies he liked the best.

The Mayor read the paper under the pie plate. 'And the winning pie for third place belongs to Etta Jones.' Her family and friends cheered for her.

'Second place goes to . . . Millie Hopkins from Hopkins Bakery.' There were also cheers for Millie.

'And first goes to . . . Cookie Parker from Cookie's Diner.' Cheers rang louder for Cookie.

'I'm sorry,' said Jenna.

'Oh well' said Millie, 'at least now we know one thing for sure.'

'What's that,' asked Jenna?

'It's not my cooking after all that draws Jake to the bakery every day'. Jenna looked a little red and a little bothered; Millie smiled and sipped her punch.

A little while later Jenna felt she had enough of Halloween, thought it was filled with more many tricks than treats. Millie was surrounded by a few of her regular customers and Jenna decided it was a good time to slip away and go home. She made an excuse to Millie about having a long day and being tired and then left.

Gertrude and Henrietta had the same idea since Jake seemed just too busy to pay any attention to them. They noticed Jenna leaving and decided the evening wouldn't be a total waste if they could poke a little more fun at poor Cinderella.

Jenna walked down the steps outside and just reached the gate when she was startled by an awful noise that resembled a burp and then horrific screams. She spun around and couldn't believe the sight that met her eyes. There was Gertrude and Henrietta lying in the mud with their feet up in the air, screeching and howling as they struggled to get back on their feet, but their big puffy dresses made it rather difficult and sanding before them was a ten foot monster, and standing beside the monster was Tyler, Matt and Billy, who were also screeching and howling, roaring with laughter. Jenna was stunned speechless. The noise of it all brought many out from the party including Mayor McGregor. 'What is going on here' he asked? The snob sisters started screaming about how Tyler and his friends scared them. Jake rushed to the scene and in one glance was able to tell what happened.

Is this true boys asked the Mayor?

Matt was silent, the Mayor, his father was really good at reading people, and he didn't think he could pull off a good, convincing lie. He never could before.

Tyler understood this and started, 'Ah . . . well . . .'

'I'm afraid it's my fault,' Jake interrupted. Every one looked at him in surprise, as Tyler and Matt breathed a sigh.

'Oh,' said the Mayor?

'Yes' said Jake, 'you see, the boys and I built this at my shop and I asked them to bring it over after everyone got tired of the spook ally.' 'I thought the little ones might like a ride in the, ah, spook wagon and Tyler Matt and Billy offered to take turns pulling them around.'

'Is that right' said the Mayor.

'Absolutely!' said Tyler, 'we just happened to be coming around the corner the same time the snob sis . . . I mean these, ah, lovely ladies were coming down the sidewalk.' Gertrude and Henrietta stood there with their mouths opened in shock.

'THAT THING ATTACKED US!!!!!!!' screamed Gertrude. Henrietta nodded frantically.

'Nonsense' said George, the chauffer for Mayor Edwards, of Richville who was waiting by the car and witnessed the whole scene. 'I saw the whole thing and it happened just like the boy said.'

Tyler Matt and Billy were in about as much shock as the snob sisters, but George had no liking for the snob sisters, and their little stunt gave him a good laugh.

'YOU WAIT TILL MY FATHER HEARS ABOUT THIS!!!!!!' cried Gertrude as they walked to the car, 'I'M

NEVER COMING BACK HERE AGAIN!!!' George walked up to Mayor McGregor who was an old friend and looked a little concerned about what Mayor Edwards might say. 'Don't worry about a thing Frank,' he said patting him on the back, they won't breath a word because if their mother ever found out they were in "poorville" as she calls it, they'd be in serious trouble. 'Richard (Mayor Edwards) will have a good laugh over this one; his only regret would be that he wasn't here to see it himself.' The Mayor smiled, 'thanks George' he said.

'GEORGE!!!!,' yelled Gertrude. George chuckled, 'I'd better get the snob sisters,' he looked at Tyler with a wink, 'I mean these lovely ladies, home'. He turned and casually chuckled his way to the car.

Matt and Tyler were so relieved but Tyler thought they were lucky that Mildred and her gang were too scared to leave their homes to come to the party or they wouldn't have gotten off so easily.

As George drove off everyone could hear Gertrude yell, 'IM FREEZING!!!' and they couldn't help laughing about it.

Jenna was grateful that everyone seemed to believe Jakes story but she knew better.

'Very well' then said Mayer McGregor, 'Jake, boys if you would like to bring your ghost in now I think there are a few goblins waiting for a ride.' 'Yes sir' said Tyler. The Mayor and the others went back into the hall.

Jenna walked up to her brother, who looked a little worried, and she gave him a big hug. 'Thank you' she said.

'What' said Tyler, 'I'm not in trouble'???

Jenna smiled, 'I appreciate what you were trying to do boys but could you please just stay out of trouble for the rest of the night?'

'Don't worry', said 'Jake I'll keep them busy'.

Jenna didn't realise he was still there. 'Oh, ah, thank you' she said. Then she turned to leave. 'Maybe Jake should walk you home', said Tyler, noticing the darkness of the night. Jenna and Jake were both surprised and embarrassed. 'He'll be too busy watching you' she said, grateful that the answer just popped into her head, 'I'll be fine' she added as she walked away.

Yes she would love it if Jake walked her home any girl in the village would have loved to have Jake walk her home but she didn't want him to do it just because her little brother asked him to.

As she walked past the huge trees that lined either side of the street she had the impression that she was not alone. She stopped suddenly when she thought she heard a rustle in the grass by the tree but when she saw nothing she decided it was just the wind and hurried on home.

Jenna walked past Tyler's room and noticed a pile of blankets on the floor by his bed. Deciding that she would make his bed for him in appreciation of what he had done for her she entered his room and saw that the green sheets she had put on his bed this morning were missing. She thought for a moment and then suddenly realised, the green monster.

But even though her sheets were ruined she couldn't possibly be angry with him.

'Oh Tyler what am I going to do with you' she said as she put a fresh set of sheets on his bed and made it up for him.

Back at the town hall the party was starting to wind down and before everyone left, Mayor McGregor was anxious to make an announcement. 'Excuse me' he said. 'If I could have your attention please, it's time to make preparations once again for the Christmas tree contest, and once again judges from the mainland will be coming to judge the village trees so I want everyone to start thinking how we can dress up our tree in center circle.

People groaned. 'That thing looks like it's about to fall over' yelled one man from the crowd.' 'Well' said the Mayor, 'I know it has seen better days but I'm told it still has a few good years left in it yet'.

'But why bother' yelled another person, 'it will be the same as every year, Richville will win'.

'You know' said another 'that we don't stand a chance against them.' The rest of the crowd agreed.

'Weather we bother or not,' replied the Mayor 'the judges are still coming and we will be decorating that tree as best we can. It's true we don't have much money in the budget for decorations so if you have any decorations you don't need or would like to sign up for the decorating committee please come up and put your name on this sheet before you leave. Thank you and happy Halloween'.

Poor Mayor McGregor was anxious to get off that stage and go home. He would come back tomorrow to see if anyone signed up and the only name he would see there would be Jakes, Millie would have liked to put her name too but with Christmas fast approaching, this was her busiest time of year.


As Jenna finished making up Tyler's bed she bumped into his telescope. Hmm she thought, why not. She looked through it and noticed that people were starting to leave the party. There was Bill Biddington and his wife Nancy who owned the fish market at the end of Main Street. A very nice couple, they always let the boys play ball in their big field behind the fish market. It was the nicest field in town; the breeze blew off the ocean and kept you cool as you played. It was also the perfect place for fireworks once a year on Pleasantville Day.

Jenna spotted Millie, Tyler and Jake. He's making sure they get home Jenna thought, how sweet.

She followed them down the street. Jake walked them to the house then she watched as he crossed the street to his own. She heard footsteps coming up the stairs and hurried to the door where she met Tyler. Oh, hi she said, I, was, just replacing the sheets on your bed.

Oh, yea, moaned Tyler, about that . . .'

'It's ok said Jenna, I think they were put to good use,' she said with a wink in her eye.

Tyler smiled and she gave him a kiss on the head and a hug, then left to go say goodnight to Millie.

Tyler set his candy bag down by the window and noticed his telescope had been moved. It was usually pointing up toward the sky but it was pointing towards . . . he thought he'd take a look, it was pointing directly at Jakes place.

He wondered why it would be, and he turned to the spot where Jenna was standing, ohh he said to himself as he put two and two together with a smile. Even though he had known both of the all of his life he had never thought of the as anything more than friends, and not really even close friends as they barely spoke to each other. But he really liked Jake and if Jenna did too, well that would be super.

Before Jenna went to bed she knelt down to pray.

'Dear Lord, I am so grateful for the wonderful people in my life, for Tyler, please bless him with the sense to stay out of trouble'. 'And Millie,' Jenna thought how she often found Millie staring at Ben's pictures in her room with tears in her eyes. Ben disappeared five years ago in the forest while searching for his brother. 'Please bless her with a heart that is healed. And . . . Jake could you please bless him with a pair of eyes to notice me? Thank you for listening, amen'.

## Chapter Two

——∾∾∾——

# Unwelcomed Guests

Saturdays were always busy days at the bakery and as usual Jenny stayed home to help Millie with the baking and the extra costumers. Some would even come from as far as Richville for Millie's cooking. Though things were sometimes hectic, they usually ran pretty smoothly. But today's business would bring a couple of unwelcomed customers.

Gertrude and Henrietta felt that they just couldn't get enough of Jake and thought perhaps today he wouldn't be so busy. Jake was on his way to the bakery for a little lunch when the snob sisters pulled up in front of his store. Unfortunately for Jake they happened to see him enter the bakery and decided to follow.

'Hi Jake said Millie, got your Saturday special right here, have a seat and I'll bring it over.' Jake sat down and Millie sat his plate on the table. 'I guess you won't be wanting any pie with that, 'she added teasing him about the pie contest.

'I'm sorry Millie', said Jake, feeling pretty bad, 'the Saturday special wouldn't be the same without your pie.'

'Oh I'm only teasing,' chuckled Millie, 'actually you did me a favour,' she said as she thought about her little conversation with Jenna. 'Jenna's got a fresh one coming out of the oven and it's just for you, I'll be right back.'

Jake wondered why choosing someone else's pie over Millie's seemed like a good thing, but his thoughts were suddenly interrupted by a high pitched squeal that made him lose his appetite.

'JAKEY POO!!!' Gertrude and Henrietta barged in and sat down on either side of him. Jake couldn't explain the cold dark feeling that came over him at the sound of that name but was beginning to feel sick now.

'We have a bit of a problem Jakey,' she moaned, 'our car died, right in front of your shop and we can't seem to get it started, perhaps you could take a look.'

Jake wanted to get the Snob Sisters out as quickly as possible so he rose and headed for the door but it was too late, Tyler Matt and Billy came in for a bite to eat as Jenna and Millie entered the bakery from the kitchen.

'Oh it's you,' said Tyler, 'thought you weren't ever coming back here.'

'Oh look,' said Henrietta, 'it's that nasty little boy, why don't you just get out?!!'

'He lives here,' said Jenna startling her from behind, 'why don't you just get out?!!!!!!!!'

'Oh my,' said Gertrude, 'this is poor Cinderella's place, I thought there was a strange smell in here.'

'Yea, well smell this,' protested Jenna as she threw Jakes pie straight at her, but she ducked and it hit Henrietta in the chest.

'AHHH she screamed.'

The customers laughed but Jenna looked furiously at Jake.

'I think it's time you took your friends out of here' she said.

'JAKE,' screeched Gertrude!!!

Jake thought once again that it was best just to make a hasty retreat. He held the door open for the girls and they left.

'And don't come back!!!' Jenna yelled as they left.

The crowd in the bakery cheered. They were not very fond of the Snob Sisters either.

Jenna politely smiled at them then furiously marched out back. Millie followed her.

'What was he thinking' snapped Jenna, 'bringing them in here expecting us to serve them after the way they treated us last night! How could he!!!'

'He didn't,'came Millie's quick reply.

Jenna was stunned and Millie saw her chance to explain.

'Jake came in alone, we had a nice little chat and he was going to have a nice little bite to eat until those two showed up.' 'He had no idea; didn't you see the look on his face?' 'All the color drained out when those two walked in.'

'Hmm' said Jenna, 'well he could have gotten rid of them.'

'But Jakes not like you, argued Millie, 'he doesn't throw pies at people, he doesn't really know how to handle people like that.'

'Well,' said Jenna a little embarrassed, 'I guess I'm not sure of the best way to handle them either but I just couldn't let them talk to Tyler like that!'

'Of course you couldn't, defended Millie, and it was great entertainment for the customers.' Jenna smiled.


Tyler Matt and Billy grabbed some food and went across the street to Jake's place. As they entered the store they heard Henrietta saying, 'and what's this tool for Jakeypoo?'

'It's a wrench,' stated Tyler, you know for when you have a few loose nuts.'

Matt and Billy laughed.

Gertrude didn't understand Tyler's reply but she knew they were laughing at her.

In order to avoid another situation like the one in the bakery Jake thought it best to separate the boys from the girls.

'Guys why don't you go out back and start dismantling the Halloween stuff and ladies perhaps I can have a look at your car.'


As the snob sisters were walking to the door Gertrude screamed when a mouse ran in front of her. She kicked it and Tyler just happened to catch it. It looked as though it were dead.

'What did you do that for he snapped?'

'It's vermin' snapped Gertrude right back.

'So are you,' replied Tyler, 'but I don't see anyone kicking you, yet.'

'Why you little' . . .

Jake hurriedly opened the door for the ladies. 'Let's take a look shall we.'

'Daddy's not going to be happy,' Henrietta fretted, 'we weren't supposed to take the car.'

'Shush!!! snapped Gertrude.

Jake and the snob sisters went out to look at the car. He first took a look under the hood. Everything seemed fine there. Then took a look inside the car and he quickly found the problem. The car had been turned off while the gear was in drive. Gertrude forgot to put it in park, or did she. Jake started up the car no problem.

'Oh you're so clever Jake,' declared Henrietta.

'Not really,' refuted Jake, 'you forgot to put the car in park.'

'Ha it wasn't me,' squealed Henrietta, as she looked at Gertrude who wanted to kick her.

'Well I was just anxious to see you Jakeypoo,' said Gertrude. Jake cringed, he really resented the nick names they gave him.


'Well if you'll excuse me I have a delivery to make,' he lied.

'We could help,' said Henrietta.

'No its ok I can handle it, ah, Mrs Wilson needs some mice traps, she has a bad mouse problem' he lied.' The girls almost jumped into their car.

Jake decided to leave while he had a chance to so he quickly went through the front door and locked it behind him. The boys were waiting for him in the back shop. Jake couldn't recall ever having told a lie but he didn't feel too bad about it.

'Are they gone,' asked Matt.

'Not yet,' said Jake, 'but I got the car going and I locked the front door, I told them I had to make a delivery of mouse traps.' The boy's chuckled.

Just then they heard a loud clap of thunder. Jake looked outside,' the sky looks pretty dark but it's not raining yet,' he said.

'Good' replied Matt I'm heading home.'

'Me too,' said Billy.

'I'd better go too' added Tyler, 'see what we can do for this little thing.'

'Give him some of Millie's stew,' said Jake, 'that will fix anything.'

'Good idea,' called Tyler as he left.

Tyler knew that Millie's stew was famous for healing all kinds of sickness. Some people would see Millie before seeing a doctor. He knew that if anything could help him it would be Millie's stew. As Tyler came around the front of the shop he saw the Snob Sisters sitting in their car trying to get the top pulled back over their heads.

'It won't budge,' complained Henrietta!

'Well go get Jake,' snapped Gertrude!

'That won't do you any good,' lied Tyler, he's gone to deliver mouse traps. Tyler laughed as he hurried home, the rain was about to start any minute. There was another loud clap of thunder as Tyler rushed into the bakery.

'Looks like you made it just in time,' said Millie. She and Jenna were looking out the front window.

'Looks like they weren't so lucky,' said Jenna pointing to the snob sisters who were getting soaked and screaming about it.

'Daddy's not going to like this,' said Henrietta.

'Oh shut up and get in,' yelled Gertrude as she started the car up again.

Tyler, Jenna and Millie had a good laugh as they watched the snob sisters drive off in their fancy convertible with the top down in the pouring rain.

Jenna noticed Tyler hanging on to his pocket.
'What's that, in your pocket?'
'A mouse' said Tyler as though it were the natural thing to have a mouse in his pocket. Millie and Jenna were a bit startled but when Tyler pulled out the poor little mouse they felt a little sympathy. 'What's wrong with him asked Millie?
'He was kicked by a Snob Sister said Tyler.
'Oh poor little thing,' said Millie, taking a closer look, 'it looks like he's still alive.'
'It looks like he's ill' said Jenna, 'I never saw a mouse with dark circles under his eyes, and he looks rather skinny for a mouse.'
'Yea, he does,' agreed Tyler hesitantly, noticing it for the first time.
'I hope it's not diseased said Jenna
'Jake says your stew would fix him right up Millie' Tyler quickly added.
'Well why don't I go and get him some,' suggested Millie.
Tyler smiled and brought the mouse up to his room. Jenna brought in a small box with an old soft rag in it, Tyler laid the mouse inside. It looked pretty sad. Millie set a little bowl of stew broth by the box. They didn't usually give mice this kind of treatment but any mouse that was kicked by a Snob Sister deserved a little T.L.C.
Once they got the mouse settled in, they went down to the kitchen to have some stew themselves. After a long day, Millie's stew was just what they needed to give them a boost of energy for the rest of the evening.

While they were enjoying their dinner, the mouse in Tyler's room was starting to stir. The aroma of the stew that Millie had set beside him had caused his nose to twitch and he opened one eye and then the other. He looked around to see where that wonderful smell was coming from and saw the tiny bowel. He managed to drag himself to the bowel and began to eat.

As the first mouthful went down he noticed a warm feeling starting to come over him so he quickly took a few more. Jenna was right, the mouse had been sick, very sick, but the warmth of this stew was quickly spreading all through his body and he could feel the pain of his sickness, which he had for months, starting to leave his body.

He finished every drop in the bowl. Now that his body finally felt at peace, he felt he could sleep for days, so he climbed back into his little bed and quickly fell asleep. A few hours later Tyler, Jenna and Millie came up to check on him.

'He looks different' said Tyler.

'Oh my, the dark circles under his eyes are gone,' claimed Jenna, and the stew is all gone.

'Oh and look, said Millie, he's even got the chubbies back into his little cheeks.'

'Jake was right,' declared Tyler, 'Jake always says your stew is good for what ails ya, Jake' . . . 'Better let him get some rest now,' said Jenna, a little tired of hearing what Jake says.

'Goodnight' she said as she kissed her brother on the head and left. Millie gave him a wink and a kiss and also left.

They all settled in for a good night's sleep.

# Chapter Three

## Terrible Tragedies

Jake, on the other hand, was not able to sleep; he lay on his bed thinking of the events of the day wishing they had gone a little different.

He thought about Jenna, and how angry she got when she saw Gertrude and Henrietta. Why did they have to show up and make it look like he invited them, that's the last thing he would do. He was very fond of Jenna.

They had gone to school together and became good friends. Jenna felt sorry for Jake and always shared her lunch with him because he rarely had one; sometimes it was the only meal of his day.

Jenna liked Jake back then because he was kind to her unlike the other boys who couldn't stand girls at that age, but Jake was just glad to have a friend. Jenna would help him with his school studies because he had no help at home, and after the tragedies, they grew even closer, for a while.

The first tragedy was when Jakes mother, Lucinda had run off with a sales man from the mainland when he was only ten years old, and only three years later his father, Ted who had a job as janitor for the town hall had disappeared with twenty thousand dollars of the towns money. He had overheard the Mayor say that they had received a late shipment of supplies and a payment of twenty thousand dollars for sale of a few boats to a mainland fishing company and since the bank would be closed the money would be locked in the safe in his office.

The town had enough fishing boats but what they desperately needed was money to fix up the one school in Pleasantville and perhaps make it a little bigger as it did hold all the grades from one to twelve. The town was excited about the new changes especially the teachers who often felt a bit cramped in small or shared classrooms. Everyone was shocked when they realised what happened. They had felt sorry for Ted when his wife ran off and since he couldn't get a job, they created a new job for him only to find that Ted escaped to the main land with their money.

In all his excitement Ted had left his mop standing next to the opened safe.

Ted liked to drink and when he did he liked to tell stories about himself.

When Jake was young he believed that his father was a wealthy explorer who traveled the world, which was why he was gone so much. Jake wondered why they lived in a little shack that was so cold in the winter, and why his clothes looked shabby compared to the other children, and why he had very little toys and none of them new.

But, as children so willingly do, he loved his father and was proud of him. He thought that if his father was so wealthy he could buy him a bicycle just like Tommy had so he asked him, Jake would never forget that day. It was the worse day of his life. Ted had been drinking and forgotten about the lies he told his son.

When Jake asked him about the bike, Ted swung his arm around and hit little Jake hard across the face. Jake landed on the floor and froze there in shock as his father yelled at him.

'Do you think I'm made of money boy?'

'Do you think I have money to throw away?'

Jake was too horrified to answer. His father grabbed his bottle and stormed out of the house.

Jakes mother who was listening in the kitchen came in and found him lying on the dirty floor but instead of comforting him and showing a little compassion she scoffed at him.

'What made you think he had money for a bike'?? The sound of his mothers voice brought him out of his shock, he thought perhaps he would find consolation.

'He said he was rich;' Jake answered, 'and went around the world and was famous'. Jake was only shocked again to find his mother laughing at him.

'You crazy fool, you believed those stories???' 'He's just a bum Jake'. She laughed and then sighed, felt a moment of sympathy for the unloved child in front of her. 'I believed his stories too.' Lucinda looked out the window as though she were seeing her past. She was eighteen and Ted was much older than Lucinda, about twelve years older, and he seemed so wise and worldly that she thought she would follow him anywhere. He was the answer to all her problems, mainly her judgemental but ailing mother.

'I left my mother on the mainland and followed him here to this God forsaken place,' she remembered the lie she told her mother about going out to dinner. She never returned and longed to be back on the mainland. Soon as I get a chance, I'm out of here'. She looked again at Jake. 'Oh don't worry Jakey, as soon as I get a place for us I'll come for you. Jake didn't know it but his mother was just as big a liar as his father was. She got her chance that night. His father was out somewhere getting drunk, a knock came at the door, Jakes mother came out in her only dress, though ten years had passed since she' set foot in Pleasantville, she still looked pretty good.

'You look nice mommy, he said.

'Oh thank you' Jakeypoo. She thought it was a compliment but it was actually a plea for her not to leave him. As he watched the stranger at the door her words ran over and over in his head, as soon as I get the chance I'm out of here.

Tears filled his eyes as he watched his mother walk towards the door. 'Mommy don't go' he cried in one last desperate plea.

She really was never much of a mother, but he didn't want to be left alone with his father.

'Oh we're just going out for dinner Jakeypoo, I'll be back.'

Jake watched out his bedroom window as she walked off with a tall stranger, knowing he'd never see her again. As he sat alone in the cold dark of his bare room the shock of all that had happened that day was becoming reality and he found his tears again. It was hours later in the middle of the night that he finally cried himself to exhaustion and fell asleep.

Jake was only eleven when this happened.

As he grew older he learned the truth, that his father was a poor fisherman, poor because he drank too much and fished too little and with all the money he had stolen he couldn't wait to hit the mainland. One night at the bar in the large city of York, he bragged on, as he liked to do when he'd had a few, about the money he had stolen right from under their noses. That night he was followed to his hotel room and the money was stolen right from under his nose as he lay there murdered in his bed.

Jenna and Jake were both thirteen when this happened. The authorities decided that Jake would have to be sent to an orphanage on the main land but Ben, Jenna's uncle, wouldn't hear of it.

Ben and his wife Millie were kind people who liked Jake and saw a lot of potential in him. He talked to the Mayor and told him that he would take care of Jake and the Mayor, who had a son of his own about that age, agreed. He knew that Ben and his family had been taking care of Jake all along.

And so Ben and Millie asked Jake to move in with them but Jake said he'd be all right on his own in the house his dad had left him. Ben and Millie's place was a small one bedroom home and Jake didn't want to intrude but the real reason was that Jake felt the weight of the shame of his parents, and he didn't want Ben or Millie to be burdened with it also. Some of his classmates wouldn't let him forget what his parents did nor would some of the town's people who gave him looks of disgust whenever they passed. Yes there were sleepless nights when Jake really appreciated the solitude of his old shack, especially after a rough day.

So it was agreed that he could stay in his house but Ben would be his guardian. Millie and Ben never had any children of their own and they both loved doteing on Jake. He was like a son to them and he did all he could to help them to show his gratitude.

Jake really didn't want to go to the main land orphanage, he now knew that both his parents came from the main land and he didn't seem to think much of the people on the main land.

Jake also felt he needed to pay back the town for the mistakes of his parents and being alone was hard enough but being alone in a strange place scared him a little, rather, a lot.

Though his shabby cold little home was filled with memories of pain and sorrow, still it was familiar to him, and became a refuge to him from the rest of the world.

There were some people, like Ben, Millie, Jenna, some of Jakes teachers and a few others who saw him for what he was, a kind, honest, mistreated child, but others judged him to be just like his parents which was unfair and hurtful at times but he could always talk to Ben when things got a little too hard to handle. Ben would say, feel sorry for those people because they got more problems than we do, that's just their way of trying to hide them, and Millie would say, 'pray for them,.' Millie believed that the Good Lord put difficult people in your path who needed someone to pray for them and perhaps you were the only person who would offer a prayer for them. Needless to say there were many souls who had no idea that a prayer had been offered up in their behalf, the man who insulted her cooking one day because his wife was with him and he couldn't say that Millies' cooking tasted better even though he thought it did, the boy who stole cookies when he thought no one was looking, even the snob sisters got a prayer or two.

Jake was so greatful to have Ben, and Ben was greatful to have Jake.

Ben was a carpenter and was doing quite well till he fell and hurt his back. There were lots of medical bills and Ben wasn't able too work as much as he use to. He and Millie had to sell their nice home and move into the much smaller one they now had, but they had eachother and they were happy. And things were picking up now because Ben brought Jake along with him on jobs that he couldn't do himself. Ben taught Jake all he knew and for the first time in his life Jake actually had money of his own.

Things were going along pretty good then one day the Mayer announced that there was going to host a dance in the town hall to help raise money for the school. Most people were pretty excited about it, especially the students. 'It sounds like a lot of fun' said Jenna, 'are you going to come?' 'Oh you're not asking him' snarled a rude voice behind her. It was Charley Stewart. He was known as one of the school bullies, his family had more money than most and he loved showing off his new toys, that he frequently received, especially infront of Jake. 'It's his fault we don't have a better school in the first place!!'

'No it isn't' protested Jenna

'Yea it is,' said Charley, 'if his dad hadn't' . . . .

'Exactly, his dad, not him!'

'Yea said Charley well he's probably just as bad. Why don't you come to the dance with me, I'll pick you up in my dads new car.

'NO THANKS!!!' Jenna abruptly turned and walked away.

Charlie then turned to Jake, 'why don't you leave her alone Jake, you're not good enough for her anyways.' He gave Jake a shove, laughed and walked off with his friends who were also laughing.

Jake learned over the years not to let people like that get to him but he sure wasn't going to pray for him; it bothered Jake when they were rude to Jenna because of him. Charlie wasn't the only one who thought Jenna was better off without him, even some of her closest and nicest friends couldn't understand why she wanted to include Jake in some of their games. He was beginning to see how the rude remarks she received about him, really bothered her. That was the day things changed. That was the moment he thought Charlie was actually right for once, Jenna would actually be better off without him. She wouldn't have to choose between him and her other friends, or suffer any more rudeness because of him. So from that day onward he became very busy in his work, often doing things for people for free especially when an event came up that he thought Jenna might invite him to.

Eventually Jenna stopped inviting him and the two slowly grew apart.

Jake thought Jenna would be happier this way and though she seemed to be because she wasn't getting hassled about him any more, she really wasn't. Jake was her best friend, Jenna could always just be herself around him. They shared their deepest secrets, they even buried a time capsule together containing Jakes favourite rock, his only marble he had found on his way home from school and his best picture he drew of Jenna. Jenna put in her lucky coin, an old school picture, a doll she use to play with and they each put in a slip of paper with their secret wishes written on it along with a few other odds and ends.

Jenna didn't understand Jakes behaviour but eventually came to accept that Jake didn't want to hang around a girl any more, he was just too busy had other interests, and so Jenna threw herself into her studies, and Jake into his work.

Jenna graduated at the top of the school with an invitation to attend the Teachers Colledge in Midville. Jake was so proud of her but yet he gave her a simple hand shake and congratulations, afraid to let his true feelings show. Jenna was almost offended at his lack of affection but she was so excited about going away to colledge, she wasn't going to let it ruin her day.

She had worked very hard for this scholarship; it was her only chance of becoming a teacher. The family bakery, although it did well enough, didn't do well enough for a colledge education but Jenna was the one student chosen this year to attend Midville College and it wouldn't cost her family anything. Jenna's family was so happy for her. It was the greatest day of her life. She'd become a teacher and life would be grand.

Over the next few years Jenna excelled in her courses and Jake excelled in his business, news had spread about his excellent carpentry skills and he was getting calls from Midville and even Richville, where there were very few carpenters if any. But Jake had a gift for carpentry and he had been taught well by Ben who now assisted him. Ben made enough money to pay off the mortage on their house and take Millie on a vacation to the mainland, it made him feel so good that his back pains disappeared.

Jake made enough money to build The Tool Barn. He also tore down his old house across the street with its bare drafty walls that held terrible memories. The Tool Barn was his own hardware store and he had his own spacious apartment upstairs and it was warm and cozy. This meant that Ben didn't have to do any more carpentry jobs which he was getting tired of after so many years; instead he helped Jake to run the store. Jake was grateful to have Ben there because he often got called away on big jobs in Richville, and Ben was grateful to have Jake whom he loved as a son.

The town was grateful to have both of them, not only because Jake presented the Mayor with a check for twenty thousand dollars to pay back what his father had stolen, but also because The Tool Barn brought in much business from Midville and even Richville, since they had no hardware stores because carpentry was considered a lesser, servant type job. Even visitors from the mainland were impressed with the store and Jakes knowledge eventhough he had never taken a trade.

Yes the town was quite greatful that only a few years ago Ben took such interest in a poor mistreated young boy that no one wanted and everyone looked down upon. They were greatful because men who came to the tool barn often brought their families along for the ride, Jake had candy machines put in for the children and had maps of the town made to hand out to the wives so they could take advantage of the time their husbands spent in the Tool Barn and visit the toy shops, dress shops and bakery.

For some it became a regular Saturday tradition to take a trip to Pleasantville which became well known for its Tool Barn, The Bakery and Priscellas Dress Shop. Yes, with all of Jakes success he certainly had enough money to move his business to Midville, perhaps even Richville and although some suggested it he certainly wouldn't think of it, he was finally happy where he was. As a matter of fact, because of his success he was beginning to feel that he was finally good enough for Jenny, but it had been so long since they had spoken that he hardly knew what to say. He accepted every job in Midville just so he might get a chance to see her while she was finishing up her last year of college, and when he did run into her all he could say was hello.

Then tragedy struck again. Jenny's parents had been invited to a wedding in Richville, her mother was really excited to go, it was one of her old school friends. The wedding was on one of the busiest days of the year, Pleasantvilles'Christmas parade day. Since the parade passed infront of the bakery several people lined up there and often came in for treats. In fact the bakery became a popular place to watch the parade from and after it was over many of the women often came in to place their Christmas order having been inspired by the parade and wanting to get an early start on their own Christmas celebrations. No the Hopkins's just couldn't afford to close shop on that day so Millie came over to help them out, and to stay with Tyler as they would only be returning the next day, which was Sunday, the bakery, like everything else, was always closed on Sunday.

After business slowed down Jenna's parents decided it was ok to go but they would have to hurry. Uncle Ben came over from the Tool Barn to stay with Millie and Tyler. He suggested they take the short cut through the forest and it sounded like a pretty good idea so they decided they would take the short cut through the forest. The road was well marked and often travelled and with their fastest horse and buggy they should make it just on time.
As they reached about the middle of the forest they heard a strange noise and stopped. It was coming from above them. They looked up to see mountains of snow falling towards them . . . they never had a chance.

No one could believe it. They had forgotten that every hundred years or so the snow became so heavy as to cause an avalanche, but only on that side of the mountain, so no one ever really worried about it, especially since it rarely ever snowed on the island.

The wedding went on as planned although it was clear there was an avalanche because it shook the whole mountain. But no one dreamed that anyone coming to the wedding would be travelling through the forest. The bride understood that the Hopkins's would be late and informed everyone to expect late arrivals. There was so much going on that no one gave the Hopkins's another thought until after celebrations were done.

But Ben did, the minute he felt the vibrations of the avalanche he knew what was happening, he looked at the clock and was horrified to realise that his brother and sister in law would not have made it out of the forest yet. Jake had the same concern and was on his way to the bakery when he saw Ben running out. They hurried to the town hall together and formed a search party.

For three days teams from all three villages searched for them without any success. There was no chance for their survival but Ben wouldn't give up, he felt it was all his fault and he couldn't bear it. Day after day he would continue his search and Jake would go with him. Ben didn't want him to because Jake had to close his shop each day, but nothing was more important to Jake than Ben was and he wasn't leaving him alone. After two more weeks of searching Ben told Jake that it was enough and he was finally giving up, but the truth was that he wanted to search another area that would take a few days journey and he would not be returning every day like they had been doing. If this journey proved unsuccessful he would then finally give up his search.

Ben had never lied to Jake before so Jake believed he was actually finished but the next morning before the dawn, Ben headed out for one last trip. It was a few hours later before Millie realised what must have happened and alerted Jake. He immediately closed up shop and went to look for him. But it was no use and so for another week the towns rescue committees searched for Ben. They found his tracks higher up the mountain but they led nowhere and then vanished.

After the committees gave up their search once more, Jake continued to search until Millie pleaded for him to stop for fear that she would loose him too. He was the only son she ever had. Jake didn't want to give up but he couldn't bear to see Millie upset any more than she was. He had to admit there was hardly a chance for survival with the little supplies that Ben took with him. So it was with a heavy heart that he stopped his search and faced the fact that he would never see Ben again. The only man who ever cared for him and rescued him from a life of misery. The one who taught him he was worth something, the one who taught him that he actually mattered, not only to him and Millie but to God.

Until Ben came along the only thing Jake knew about God was that he was the person you blamed when things go wrong as his parents often did. It never made much sense to Jake to blame an invisible person for your own mistakes. Until Ben came along Jake didn't believe in God. He couldn't believe that a great being could make a child suffer. The only ones he blamed were his parents. But Ben and Millie taught him that there was a God and that he loved children and all people. They showed Jake how He blessed the lives of many people and how God blessed his own life. Now that Jake believed in God he decided that all he could do was leave it in His hands.

Jake returned to his shop but it was still a few weeks before he opened the doors to the public. He just couldn't face people as though nothing had happened, it would take time.

A week later a representative from the Midville nursing home came to him asking for help, the building was in serious need of repair and renovation, health officials were threatening to shut it down if changes weren't made soon, and many of the residents had nowhere else to turn. Of course Jake couldn't say no and after he got started, he found that he was grateful to have something to keep his mind busy.


Millie stayed at the bakery to care for Tyler though the shop remained closed.

Jenna finished up her schooling a few weeks later but instead of attending the graduating ceremonies and celebrations as she had dreamed of doing over the past year especially, she just came home and Millie made her a special dinner. Jenna couldn't face graduation without her parents there. They were her best friends and her main support group. It was a celebration they had planned together. She picked up her diploma at the Deans office, who was very understanding and she went home. Jenna really didn't have an appetite but she could tell that Millie went through a lot of work preparing this special meal and she didn't want to ruin it for her.

It was decided at this dinner that Millie should stay and she and Jenna could run the bakery since there were no openings for a teacher at the moment. Life slowly started moving forward again and a few changes were made on the way. Millie sold her house and with the money she received she made some renovations to the bakery. The front of the bakery was extended, as her sister always wanted, and there were now a few tables and chairs by the windows for those who liked to rest and enjoy a piece of pie or some of Millie's stew which was quickly becoming famous, well on the island anyway.

Millie also bought new bakery supplies and appliances, which made the cooking and bakeing much faster and easier. Millie had more time to relax with customers, even after Jenna got the exciting call to teach eighth grade at Pleasantville Jr. High. She didn't want to leave Millie but Millie insisted, she pretty much ran the show anyways. This is what your parents dreamed about she insisted; now you go and make them proud. Jenna was a great teacher, she had a way with children and the school was glad to have her. After her first year she got a call from Midville High, offering her a teaching position with higher pay but she turned it down to stay with Millie and Tyler.

Jake was so glad that Jenna didn't take the job in Midville. Everything was settling down and becoming peaceful again that is until Gertrude and Henrietta showed up.
The thought of them jolted Jake back to the present. Why did they have to come, he thought, and ruin everything.
Jake tried to put them out of his mind and get some sleep but all he did was toss and turn. He looked at the clock it was two a.m. I have to sleep he told himself, tomorrow is Saturday and Saturday's are always busy.

# Chapter Four

## Tragedies Continued

Suddenly the phone rang, it was Ole Pete at the light house and he was frantic.

'Lightening has struck the light house, I was nearly fried in my boots he screeched,' 'It's a miracle the down stairs phone still works but the light is gone and theres a ship out there due in about three thirty.' 'I called the Mayor, he continued, there are no replacement lights left and he said the new shipment of lights are suppose to be on that boat. How do you like that!!!' 'I don't have any lights here bright enough,' said Jake, 'but I'll bring what I have, at least the rain has stopped, we'll need to build a huge fire call the mayor again and tell him to sound the alarm, we need to get as much dry wood as we can.' 'Alright' said Pete.

Jake quickly dressed and loaded his truck with flashlights and all the spare wood he could find he also grabbed a jug of gasoline. Everyone was soon awakened by the loud piercing noise of the town hall siren.

Jenna and Millie ran to Tyler's room and found him looking out the window through his telescope. What is it, said Jenna. I hope it's not a fire said Millie. It looks like the whole town is running to the town hall said. We'd better go too said Millie someone must be in trouble. They grabbed their coats and flashlights and headed for the door. Tyler noticed on his way out that the little mouse bed on the table was empty but he'd have to worry about that later. Jenna opened the door as Jake was driving by. He quickly stopped when he saw the door open. Would you like a lift he asked? We're only going to the town hall said Jenna, looking a little disturbed. The problem is at the light house, said Jake, we could use your help. Tyler Millie and Jenna got in and off they went. Jake explained on the way that lightening had hit the lighthouse. It wasn't too badly damaged but the light wasn't working and old Pete, who lived in the light house couldn't get it to work and there was a ship expected in. They needed a huge bonfire on the shore, tall enough for the ship to see. The town's people were gathering their wood supplies but there was already a stack of it at the light house and if they worked together they could get a fire started quickly and they could just add the wood that the others brought as it came.

Ole Pete apologised to Jake when they arrived, 'but it was kind of urgent' he said. Jake told Pete that he couldn't sleep anyway.

'Can anyone hear me' came a frantic voice from the down stairs radio. Pete and Jake both rushed into Petes little house attached to the light house, the others quickly followed. Pete grabbed the radio. 'Hello we're here can you hear me' he cried. 'Yes' came the reply, 'were in trouble were grounded on some rocks and were taking on water.' 'We couldn't see the lighthouse.' 'No' said Pete, 'the lightening took out the light, do you have any idea where you are asked Jake.' 'I can't see anything but a wall of rock' replied a worried voice. 'I think I know where you are said Jake its not far about 15 minutes I'm on my way.'

Jake grabbed the keys off the hook by the door; they belonged to the towns only search boat tied up at the dock. 'I want to come' cried Tyler. 'No!!' said Jake and Jenna together firmly, as they gave eachother a quick glance. 'I need you here' said Jake 'we need a big fire there's dry wood in the back of my truck, get it started before everyone else gets here.' Normally Jake would never put Tyler in charge of a fire but he wanted to make Tyler feel important and knew he would be supervised and Millie and Jenna understood.

Jake ran on to the boat and Tyler, Millie, Jenna and Pete got busy with the fire. Soon others had arrived and they had a nice huge bon fire on the beach, under Tyler's direction of course.

Jake was a volunteer fire fighter and search and rescue, it wasn't long before Jake found the stranded ship. He was glad to see it wasn't sinking quickly because of the many rocks, and everyone was ok but he had to keep his distance or be stranded himself. So Jake anchored and lowered the row boat. It was no problem to row the little boat over to the ship.

'Are we ever glad to see you' said Will, the captain as he helped Jake on to the ship. 'I'm glad to see you too' said Jake, 'are you still takeing on water?' 'Some,' replied Will, 'but I don't think she'll be going anywhere soon.'

Just then the ship tilted a little as it slipped on the rocks throwing everyone off balance.

'Then again I could be wrong.'

Do you have any injured asked Jake hanging on to a pole, we should take them first. The ship was a little slanted but they were able to get most of the crew off of the ship, Jake rowed back and forth several times, but the crew were too wet, cold and weak to help out so Jake never mentioned how sore and exhausted he was getting.

The ship carried a few more men than the little rescue boat could; there wasn't enough room for everyone. Jake decided he would stay behind and gave directions to Nick, one of the ship's crew who was also another search and rescue volunteer who knew his way around the waters, and they left. Will and four others remained on the boat to wait for their return.

The town cheered as they saw the boat approaching the shore but became silent as they watched the crew move quickly to safely get the injured to shore.

'Where's Jake,' cried out Tyler? 'He, and a few others had to remain behind' explained Nick, 'there wasn't enough room for everyone, we're going back for them now.' 'We'll wait for you,' said Pete, the rest of you fella's are cold and tired why don't you go on home?' All of the crew refused to go home with their families, even the injured, refused to be taken away. 'Is there something you're not telling us, asked Pete?' The crew looked at eachother and decided that they deserved to know the truth. 'The ship has taken on a lot of water and was slowly sinking, said Nick, but I'm sure they'll make it.'

Jenna put her arm around Tyler who looked worried and angry. She too was worried about Jake when she didn't see him and was glad when she heard Tyler call out, 'where's Jake,' because she really wanted to know, though she'd never admit it.

The crowd waited anxiously, some silently praying and some silently weeping. This was taking longer than it should have and ships had been sunk there before.

Finally they saw the rescue boat coming and cheered as they watched as it docked. But only two people came forth, Nick and Jim, another member of the crew who had returned with him for the search. They saw the crowd approaching, Tyler in the lead.

'Where's Jake' he yelled the minute he noticed that Jake was missing.

'I'm afraid we were too late, said Nick. The ship was gone. It looked like it had broken into pieces; we searched the waters but tides come in, we couldn't find them anywhere, I'm sorry,' Nick said with tears in his eyes.

Tyler couldn't believe his ears; it felt like his very breath had been taken out of him. We need more rescue ships said the Mayor, were not giving up, you two get some rest we'll get another crew out.

I'll go, piped up one man from the crowd, a couple more followed him to the boat. 'I want to go too,' cried Tyler, desperately, to Jenna. 'I know said Jenna,' whose heart was thumping,' but I have a better idea come with me' she walked away from the crowd. Tyler followed her although doubtfully, he thought she was just saying that to get him away from the boat, but then he became confused as he saw her walk towards Jake's truck.

'I'm not going home' Tyler protested.

'Neither am I' said Jenna.

'What are you going to do' asked Millie who was also following quickly behind wipeing her tears? 'They said they searched the water' said Jenna. 'Yea, so,' said Tyler shortly. 'So, said Jenna I can't see Jake just standing there waiting for the boat to go down can you?'

'No, but . . .'

'The captain said there was a wall of rock but they didn't mention searching the wall, said Jenna, I know where it is she said as she climbed into the truck and started it. Tyler quickly followed, Jenna didn't have the heart to tell him no, she just nodded.

'Be Careful said Millie.' In her heart she wanted to go too but she knew they would need the rest of the space for the men if they found them. 'I'll have some stew waiting.'

'We'll be back as soon as we can,' assured Jenna. As she quickly drove off she noticed Tyler wipeing a tear but didn't say a word knowing that he was trying to be brave.

Soon they came to the edge of of a cliff. Jenna left the lights on and grabbed a large flashlight that was left lying on the seat. She and Tyler hurried to the edge of the cliff and shone the light down. 'Hello yelled Jenna is anyone there!!!! 'Jake, yelled Tyler are you there!!!! There was no reply. They looked at each other in dispare. It's a big cliff said Jenna lets try further down. They got back in the truck and drove a little further down. They tried again, and again with no success. They've got to be somewhere stated Jenna as she noticed the frightened look in Tylers face. Come on were not giving up this easy she added, there's one more spot. Tyler was doubtful as Jenna drove on and bit his lip forcing himself to hold back the tears.

After about ten minutes of strenuous silence they finally arrived. Tyler dragged himself to the cliff trying to prepare for another failure.

He just stood there holding the rope as Jenna yelled 'Hello!!! anyone down there?'

'Help!!!' Jenna and Tyler were so shocked to actually hear a reply; they were stunned for a moment as tears welled up in their eyes.

'Jake!!!' cried Tyler.

'Tyler is that you' Jake called.

'Me and Jenna' said Tyler.

'Is everyone alright' asked Jenna?

'We're ok,' said Will, 'but it's impossible to climb, the tide came in and we almost went down with the ship but we grabbed on to the rocks and climbed halfway up the wall but were stuck here on this ledge and the water's getting higher, we saw the rescue boat but they couldn't hear us and they couldn't come any closer for the rocks.' Tyler wiped his eyes and quickly went to tie one end of the roap to the truck.

'Did you bring anyone with you yelled Charlie,' one of the crew.

'No' called Jenna who recognised that voice as the same Charlie from school who was such a bully.

'Great we're wet cold, wet and exhausted' stomped Charlie angrily 'and doomed to die here on these rocks because we can't be rescued by a girl and a boy.'

'Excuse me!?' Jenna was angry as Tyler threw down the end of a rope. Jake did you get it he yelled. 'Good job' said Jake.

'A fat lot of good that's gonna do' said Charlie 'they'll never be able to pull us up.'

'Who's that' asked Tyler to Jenna?

'You could always wait for the rescue boat said Jenna its making another trip.'

'Were all set' said Jake, 'were sending Tommy up first.'

Jenna ran to the truck and slowly backed it up while Tyler kept watch on Tommy to see that he wasn't coming up too fast. How's she doing it, asked Charlie, who couldn't believe his eyes.

'She has my truck' answered Jake.

'You don't think they walked all the way here in the dark do you' asked Will?

Charlie was too embarrassed to answer. 'I'm next' he demanded.

'No you're not' said Will, 'Donald is, then Jake then you then me.'

'I'll go last said Jake, the waters coming up fast and I'm the tallest.'

Will wanted to argue but his head only came to everyone elses shoulder and the water was almost to his waist. He just nodded.

Jake's hands were numb as he finally tied the rope around his own waist which was under water by this time and he wasn't sure it would hold.

Jake was almost to the top and could feel the rope slipping. Just as he reached the top it let go and he slid down before anyone could grab him. Luckily Jake was able to grab the large knot at the end of the roap and hang on. His hands scraped along the rocks and were bleeding but he managed to hang on till they pulled him up.

Jenna was so relieved to see him.

When the rope had slipped she felt a jerk in tension and thought she lost him till the others motioned for her to keep backing up.

Once he was up she drove the truck back to the men and saw he was still lying on the ground.

'Jake are you ok?' she anxiously asked, 'I'm sorry . . .

'No it wasn't your fault Jenna,' he said as the others helped him up, 'I couldn't tie the roap tight enough, my hands were too cold.'

Jenna looked at his hands, 'Oh Jake,' she said, 'common let's get you fixed up.'"

As they walked to the truck they noticed Charlie sitting in the front on the passenger's side. 'Is there even a heater in this old thing?!'

That did it, Jenna had lost all sense of patience and manners and before Will could say anything she grabbed Charlie and pulled him out of the truck. 'Get the hell out of this truck,' she demanded, as he landed on the ground. Tyler's eyes couldn't have been any bigger as his ears couldn't believe that his perfect, proper sister could ever say or do anything like that.

'You should have been the last one up' she went on, 'not Jake, you're always bragging about how tough you are.

'Charlie? Tough?' said Will, 'he's the biggest whiner I've ever had on my ship.'

'You either get in the back or you can walk, ordered Jenna, Will and Jake will sit in the front.'

'Oh and one more thing' said Will, 'you're fired.'

As they drove off Will asked, 'ever think of working on a ship Jenna? You'd make a good captain.'

Soon everyone was delivered to their homes and the rescue boat was called off. Ole Pete was glad to hear that Jake was ok.

At last it was just Jenna Tyler and Jake in the truck. 'I should take you to the hospital Jake,' said Jenna.'
'No need said Jake, my hands aren't broken I'll be fine.'
'Well at least come to our place and let Millie fix you up.'
'Ok,' said Jake. Millie couldn't stop the tears when she saw them, she thought she'd lost another member of the family, but before long she had Jake fixed up with bandaged hands and a hot bowl of stew, and Tyler had run over to Jakes place and got him some dry clothes. Jake was so greatful for wonderful friends. As Jake finished his last spoon full Millie asked if he would like another bite.
'No I'm fine now, said Jake, thanks to you, all of you. I think I'd better go home and get some rest.'
'Nonsense you should stay here,' insisted Millie. 'There's an extra bed in Tyler's room' said Jenna, hoping she didn't sound too eager.
'Yea' said Tyler excitedly, he never thought he'd have Jake for a sleep over.
'That sounds good' Jake relented, though he didn't want to be a bother, he was too tired to argue.

As they entered Tyler's room Jake noticed the little mouse bed. 'What's this' he asked?
'Oh that was the little mouse bed, the mouse that snob sister kicked, we layed him in there and gave him some of Millies stew and now hes gone.'
'Probably went to get some more stew' smiled Jake. Tyler gave a little laugh.
'Hey Tyler, I could never thank you enough for what you did tonight.'
Jenna walked in with extra blankets.
'It was Jenna`s idea to to check the rocks, said Tyler.

'Jake and Jenna looked at each other.

'Thank you' said Jake 'we would have been . . . gone.

Jenna nodded. 'Here are some extra blankets; it can get drafty in this old house at night.' 'Everyone all set' asked Millie, as she came in to say goodnight?

'All set,' affirmed Tyler.

'Yes, thank you' said Jake.

'Good,' said Millie, 'now everyone come here,' she said as she held out her hands to her sides. She took Jake's hand on one side and Jenna's on the other.

'What happened here tonight was a miracle and we need to be grateful.' Tyler joined the ring as Millie bowed her head.

'Dear Lord, we have so much to be grateful for, our hearts are over flowing with gratitude for the magnificent blessings that thou hast bestowed upon us this night.' 'We thank thee for protecting Pete when lightening struck the light house.' 'We thank thee for all the kind hearted people of this town who came to the rescue sacrificed and served tonight to build a huge fire.' 'We thank thee for Jake,' Millie's voice quivered as she fought back the tears so she could finish her prayer, 'for guiding him to those poor stranded souls on the ship, nearly sacrificing his own life so that others may be saved.' She needed a moment to recompose. 'And we thank thee Lord for Jenna and Tyler, for they never gave up.' 'We thank thee for guiding them to Jake and the others so that they may be rescued from a watery grave.' Millie's tears won over this time, she put her hands to her face; 'I'm sorry' she cried into Jake's arms.

'Its ok' said Jake, we're all safe now.

Jenna was grateful that Jake was such a comfort to Millie; she understood that to Millie, Jake was just as much family as she and Tyler were. Jake also meant a lot to her. She hoped no one noticed her blinking back a tear now and then through the prayer; she also would have been devastated if he were lost, as would Tyler. In fact she didn't know who would have missed him the most, Millie who loved him as a son, Tyler who loved him as a big brother, or Jenna herself who deep down inside always loved him and now she could almost forgive him for his little escapade with the snob sisters. Tyler joined in the group hug and so did Jenna. She realised that Jake was very kind hearted, too kind hearted at times and but she just expected him to stand up for her against the snob sisters. She did after all stand up for him against Charlie, many times but Jakes early childhood years gave him no reason to develop courage or even self confidence. He was often belittled at school and at home, it wasn't untill Ben and Millie came into his life that he began to realise his own self worth, but the habits of self doubt were deeply instilled and something that he would always struggle with.

Jenna, on the other hand was raised by loving, supportive parents who gave her every opportunity and confidence to achieve and excel, which gave her the courage to stand up for herself and others, but more important they gave her love.

Deep down inside Jake always believed she was worth far more than he was for many reasons but one of them being that she was so smart. He believed that people who worked in banks or offices or schools were some how better than people who didn't understand all of that brainy stuff because they weren't smart enough.

He didn't believe that everything he could do was anything special, eventhough he earned more money than most people working in offices, banks, or schools. What he did just came natural to him and he enjoyed it. It didn't seem much like work to him hand he didn't consider it anything spectacular even though he was often praised as the best carpenter around.

What Jake didn't realise was that if you could make a good living at something that you really loved, that was the smartest idea of all. He also didn't realise that many of those stuck at a desk all day working for someone else, were highly stressed and not very happy.

## Chapter Five

———❧———

# Another Rescue or Two

Everyone slept well, everyone except for Millie that is, who tried but at 5:00 a.m. her internal clock demanded, it was time to get up so she threw on her robe and headed to the kitchen.

Only one short hour after they had finally gotten to their beds was everyone woken up, but not by the usual marvellous aroma of Millie eggs and bacon that always drew a crowd, nor was it by the wonderful scent of Millie's Rise and Shine Cinnamon buns that made your mouth water. But it was the piercing sound of Millies voice as she screamed that made everyone jump out of their beds and run to the kitchen. The sight that stood before them was something never before seen. Millie stood frozen on the spot as did the mice, about a hundred of them.

Tyler looked at Millie and then he looked at the mice. 'Wow' he said.

And then something miraculous happened, one of the mice, by the name of Gregory, began to speak.

'Please' he said, 'we mean you no harm' at which point Millie was about to faint but Jake caught her and put her in a chair.

'You, you speak' asked Jenna?

'Yes' said Gregory 'but'...

'Do all mice have the ability to speak,' she interrupted.

'No, only those of us from the mountain he replied.'

'Hey I know this mouse' said Tyler, 'you're the one I brought home.'

'Yes Tyler' said Gregory, 'and I can't thank you enough for that, you see were not suppose to speak to people but these

51

are desperate times, and we have no choice, we need help, we don't want to bother anyone but . . .'

'What can we do' asked Jake?

'We are being killed by a disease,' said Gregory sadly.

'What disease' ask Jenna with a lot of concern?

'It's called . . . it's called . . . well I can't remember the name of it, answered Gregory, it's not harmful to humans, he added noting their look of concern, but it seems to attack every hundred years or so and nearly wipes us clean out. We don't know how it comes or how it goes, but now we know how to treat it.'

'How asked Jenna?

'Well thanks to you we now have the antidote' said Gregory.

'You do' asked Tyler?

'Yes of course, declared Gregory, it's the medicine you gave me last night.'

'Medicine' asked Tyler, you mean Millie's stew?'

'Whatever you call it' said Gregory, 'just the smell of it was bringing me back to my senses and at the first taste of it I could feel its warmth spreading through my whole body, healing me, I had to get more, I had to get help before it was too late.' 'If you could spare us a little more we would be forever in your debt. Tyler, Jenna and Jake didn't answer right away; they were amazed that chicken stew could do so much.

'And forever grateful' added Gregory still hoping it wasn't too much to ask for.

Millie found her voice and her strength; she went to the fridge and pulled out a big pot.

'Will this be enough she said, you can have it all and I can make more, as much as you need.' The mice were stunned, their little eyes nearly popped out of their heads. Jake, Jenna, and Tyler were also surprised but Millie ignored them and went on, 'I'll warm some up to give you strength for your journey back.'

Before long the mice were as good as new and just about ready to return. Jenna was filling the last little mouses bottle with the stew broth.

'I have a question' she said.

'Yes' said Gregory.

'You said the disease was not harmful to humans.'

'Yes that's right' said Gregory.

'How do you know?'

'Yea said Tyler, how do you know?'

'Teacher is human' said Gregory.

'Your teacher' asked Jenna?

'He is wonderful, he taught us how to speak' . . . .

'What's your teacher's name' asked Jake?

'Why do you ask? I told you his name is Teacher, said Gregory.

'Well, here a teacher is a job title said Jenna.'

'Yea' said Tyler 'Jenna's a teacher but we call her Jenna.'

Gregory's eyes grew big. 'You're a teacher???' he asked.

'Yes' said Jenna unsure.

'Oh' said Gregory as he bowed and all of his mice followed, 'we are honoured.'

Now everyone was confused.

'Oh my,' exclaimed Jenna, 'I wish I got that kind of respect at school,' she looked at Tyler who smirked and sarcastically bowed.

Jenna turned her attention back to Gregory, 'it's an honor to meet you too she claimed.'

'It is' asked Gregory confused?

'Definitely' said Jenna, 'we've never met mice who had such intelligence'. 'Yea'said Tyler, mostly they just steal our food and poop in our cupboard.'

One of the mice in the crowed looked suspiciously guilty but no one noticed.

George chuckled a bit, 'Teacher will be waiting for this; we really must go.'

'Will these tiney bottles be enough for everyone' asked Millie concerned?

'No' said Gregory 'I'm afraid not, but it's a start and we can come back for more.'

'But' said Jake 'by the time you get back here again . . .'

'I know,' said Gregory, 'some of us might die.'

'We can help' blurted out Tyler.

'Yes let us help you' added Jenna.

'It's too far said one mouse,' 'too risky' stated another.

'You can't fit through the tunnels' said one more mice.

'How did your teacher get there' asked Jenna.

'She is smart, said a mouse, she must be a teacher.'

'I want to be a teacher' said a little girl mouse.

'But' piped up another 'no peoples is allowed.'

'No people are allowed,' corrected Jenna.

'She sounds just like teacher' exclaimed the little girl mouse, 'we should trust her.'

The little group of mice huddled together, finally Gregory spoke. 'It's decided, they will go back through the tunnels and I will take you there, through the woods.

In just a few seconds all of the mice but Gregory were gone. 'It's a long trip back your way' said Gregory, 'there are tunnels all over this mountain and they are much faster.'

'But don't you live in the forest' asked Tyler?

'Well the entrance is there, we live, in the mountain and the avalanche we had years ago destroyed some of the tunnels leading here but I finally found a way out.

'The avalanche also took our parents' said Tyler, 'and Uncle Ben.'

'Oh how terrible' said Gregory, 'I'm so sorry.'

'The road has since been repaired' said Jenna trying to stay focused.

'Do you think you could get us there from here, added Jake?

'Certainly' said Gregory eagerly.

'Good' said Jake, 'I'll put this in the truck' he added grabbing the pot.

'I'll make some more,' said Millie, intent on doing all she could now that she was almost over the shock of having talking mice in her kitchen. Tyler held out his hand for Gregory to walk on and he put him in his front pocket. You must come too, Teacher, Jenna,' said Gregory, everyone looked at Jenna, 'Teacher will want to meet you.'

'I wouldn't miss it' replied Jenna, I would like to meet teacher too.'

Quickly they were on their way and soon they came to a fork in the road.

'You must turn right here' said Gregory.

'But this road doesn't lead any where' said Jake as he turned.

'Yes that's what the people think' said Gregory as he yawned, 'excuse me he said, it's been a long night.'

'Intelligent and polite' said Jenna as she smiled at Gregory who blushed a little.

The road led up the mountain but eventually came to an end and Jake stopped the truck and everyone got out.

'Where do we go from here asked Tyler?'

'It's grown over quite a bit,' said Gregory, 'but I believe it's straight ahead.' The sun was now coming up which made it easier for them to see, they were grateful for that because it was quite difficult to push their way through the bushes, even more difficult for Jake carrying the pot of stew.

'It looks like weve climbed about half way up the mountain' said Jake.

Are you sure you know where were going asked Tyler?

'Yes yes' said Gregory excitedly, just a little bit farther.

After another half hour of trudging they came to a large rock jutting out from the face of the mountain, and beside the rock was a narrow opening.

There it is said Gregory with excitement.

'Wow said Tyler amazing' he exclaimed!

'I'm afraid the hole isn't very big' said Gregory 'but inside is much bigger.'

After everyone climbed through the hole they were able to stand up.

They had hoped it would be easier once they got inside the mountain but were sorely mistaken.

They were standing on a little ledge on the inside wall of the mountain that wound around and led to the bottom. One slip and it would be over.

There was a little light coming from outside but it was difficult to see.

'I didn't know we would be going inside the mountain,' said Jake, 'I didn't bring any flashlights.'

'Flashlights' asked Gregory?

'Like this' said Tyler as he pulled a small flashlight out of his pocket, along with his assorted pocket knives and a couple of rare bottle caps.

'Ingenious' said Gregory, 'but no need for that' he said as he scurried over the wall of the mountain. It seemed to be covered with roots of some sort. Suddenly the walls around them lit up.

'Amazing' said 'Jenna how did you do that.'

'Well its simple' said Gregory, 'you just have to find the proper root and give it a tweak.'

'Oh yea,' smiled Jenna, 'simple.'

'It's this way' said Gregory.

'It's no wonder no one has found this place' said Jenna, be careful Tyler she added you could fall'.

'Teacher found this place' said Tyler ignoring his sister.

'Yes' said Jake 'how did he find it?'

'He fell' said Gregory, as he scurried off.

Every few meters Gregory would tweek some more roots and lights their path a little further.

'How far is it to your'ah, . . . Tyler didn't know what to call it.

'Village' said Gregory.

'Village . . .'

'VILLAGE?!!'

'Of course Jenna; the missing village!'

'People thought it was only a legend, the book said it was in the forest, the inhabitants were small and they had great riches, are you rich Gregory?'

Gregory chuckled, 'our ancestors did live in the forest but they too experienced a major avalanche and the survivers moved into the mountain weve been here ever since. But I don't know about the great riches.'

'Perhaps it's these lights they were talking about' said Jake.

'Maybe said Tyler but I figured it out, teacher, he said to Jenna, the mystery of the fourth village, I should get some extra points for that!'

'Yes I suppose you should,' confirmed Jenna, 'but you still have to do your writing piece.'

Tyler smiled and nodded.

'Wow exclaimed Tyler, is this the village?' He pointed to many large mushrooms about two feet high.

'It used to be, said Gregory, until teacher came and made us better houses that wouldn't die, these only last a little while, they made good shelters, but we had to keep moving from one to the other.'

As they walked on they had to be careful because there were many narrow ridges easy for a mouse to walk on but barely big enough for a persons' foot. Jake had thought it a bit difficult to carry a pot of stew through the bushes outside but this was much harder. Soon they came to a larger opening that was already lit up. There was a little stream with a tiny little bridge and on the other side of the stream, which Jake, Jenna and Tyler could just walk over, there was a tiny village scattered with small wooden houses.

'Look at that' cried Tyler. 'That's our village' said Gregory.

'Oh it's beautiful' said Jenna, looking at all the coloured houses.

'But where's everyone' asked Tyler, maybe they're afraid of us, here mousy, mousy.'

'Mousy, mousy??' George laughed.

'They're all up at teacher's house.'

'There's something strange about this place' said Jake as he set the pot down and took a closer look. 'These houses, they're exact replicas of Plesantville, look there's the town hall, and the bakery there's the Tool Barn he said, getting down on his knees to take a closer look, even the door is made exactly the way Ben and I' . . . He looked from the door to Jenna. 'We'd like to see your teacher they both suddenly said together.'

'Of course said Gregory, a bit confused, his house is just over that hill.' They quickly pressed on and soon saw a large house. It seemed so strange that for a moment they forgot they were in the middle of a mountain.

'I don't know this house' said Tyler puzzled. 'I do' said Jake. Jenna was puzzled too and was about to ask Jake when . . .

'WAIT' Tyler yelled to Gregory!!!

'What' said Gregory as he turned to see Tyler pointing to a large white cat with three legs.

'Is that the reason your village is empty?!'

'Oh you mean Duchess asked Gregory no she's our protector.'

'Protector from what' asked Jenna a little concerned?

'Weasels, answered Gregory, 'but don't worry there haven't been any here for a long time.'

He rang a bell near the bottom of the door and when the door opened, there stood a tall man with a long grey beard and kind, blue eyes. Tyler noticed that Jake, and Jenna were stunned at the sight of him. 'What's wrong he whispered.'

'Please come in said the man, you must be tired.'
'These are your friends Gregory?'
'Yes said Gregory who was standing on a hall table, this is Tyler and this is Jake oh and this is Teacher Jenna and she's very smart too.' 'A teacher' said the man pleased. Jenna was speechless she just shook her head. 'Ah, here's the medicine we brought' said Jake showing the pot to the man.
'Oh marvalous said the man I didn't expect so much.' 'The others arrived a short while ago and told me to expect your arrival but of course they could only carry a little bit and I've already administered it and there is still much to do please excuse me.' and with that he was gone.
Jenna and Jake looked at each other.
'What is the matter with you two' asked Tyler?
'It was him wasn't it' said Jenna.
'Yes I'm positive' said Jake, and this is his house, the one he and Millie lived in before . . . .'
'Of course' said Jenna it's really him.
'WHO!!!' demanded Tyler, growing impatient?
'Uncle Ben' answered Jenna.
Tyler searched his memory back to when he was eight. 'That was him' he said, 'why didn't he say so?'
'He doesn't seem to remember us' she answered sounding a little disturbed, it must have been that fall.
'Gregory, was there anyone with him, are there any other people here?'
'No, I'm afraid not he replied, you thought maybe your parents? . . . I'm sorry.'
'It's alright said Jenna, at least we've found Uncle Ben but what will we tell Millie.'
'We'll just tell her the truth' said Jake.

Jenna nodded, 'Gregory could you take us to where Uncle . . . I mean, Teacher is, perhaps we can help.'
'Of course' answered Gregory.

They followed him to a door at the end of the hall. Once again they were amazed by what layed before them. There were several tables and on the tables it seemed that there were about a hundred tiney hospital beds. A few of the mice noticed the visitors and started to panic, soon the whole room was in a panic.
'Calm down said Teacher these are our friends they brought us the medicine.'
'We just thought maybe we could help, said Jenna, we certainly didn't mean to scare anyone, I'm really sorry.'
'They're allright said Teacher, actually I could use a little help.'
'Sure said Jake what can we do?'
'If you could fill these bowls and lay them beside the beds on those last three tables that would save me a lot of time' answered Teacher.
The little mice were so grateful that they quickly warmed up to their new visitors. Soon the task was completed and the mice were left to their own, to get some rest.
Everyone returned again to the front room. 'My friends didn't say where you were from do you come from the camp site, asked Teacher?'
'Camp site' asked Jenna?
'Yes said Teacher look I drew a map of the mountain.' He pointed to a map on the wall, 'It's up here,' he showed them a spot on the map high up on the mountain.
'No were not from there' said Jake.
'Good said Ben, because every summer people camp there and, well, I've borrowed a few things from them over the years he added motioning to his clothes.'

Jenna smiled as she walked over to the map, we're from here' she said as she pointed to the bottom of the mountain. 'Oh said Teacher, Iv'e never gone down the mountain, only up.'

'Have you never wanted to go down' asked Jenna.

'I've often thought about it said Ben but then I . . . well I just get the feeling that going down the mountain would be, painful in some way so I've never gone, is it nice there?'

It's wonderful said Jenna there are so many wonderful things about being there, you . . . used to live there she added cautiously.'

'What' asked Ben thinking she must be mistaken?

'It's called Pleasantville' added Jake.

Ben still looked confused.

'If you don't remember asked Tyler, how did you build the mouse village? It looks just like Pleasantville.'

'It does' asked Teacher?

'Don't you remember us Uncle Ben' asked Tyler exasperated.

Teacher looked at them all curiously, 'you say I'm your uncle' he asked?

'Well Tyler's and mine said Jenna, but you're like a father to Jake, or you were.'

Ben remembered something, wait here a minute he said as he rushed out of the room.

'Do you think he's ok asked Tyler?'

But before anyone could answer Ben quickly returned with something in his hand, it was a picture.

'Do you know this person' he asked?

'Aunt Millie' exclaimed Tyler.

'Millie' asked Ben?

'You don't remember her either' groaned Tyler? Ben sadly shook his head no.

'Your name, said Jenna is Benjamin, Joseph Hopkins, Millie is your wife and you have been missing for five years.'

Ben was trying to take this all in and understand it, he walked over to his map. 'Did I not like it there, Did I . . . not like her.'

'You were very happy together affirmed Jake you loved it there.'

'Then why did I leave' asked Ben a little exasperated himself?

'This is the hard part said Jenna, you were right, going back down would cause you pain but . . .

'I must hear it' said Ben.

'You left to find our parents, Tyler's and mine, they were, killed, in an avalanche, my father, Gregory, was your brother.' 'Do you remember any of that? Ben shook his head no.

'Well you remembered the name Gregory,' said Jenna encouragingly. 'That's my name' stated Gregory.

'You must be a special mouse smiled Jenna, because Ben and my father, Gregory, were very close. Gregory smiled proudly not realising what all of this could mean.

You and Jake searched for them for weeks, long after the towns search committee gave up. You promised Millie you wouldn't search any more, every time you went out even though you knew there was no chance for their survival after a week, she was afraid you wouldn't return and every time you came back more broken up inside because you couldn't bear the pain.

You told everyone you were finished searching but the next morning you left Millie a note saying there was one more spot you wanted to check out and you were gone before anyone knew. Jake spent the next three weeks looking for you, till Millie pleaded for him to stop before she lost him too.

Ben looked at the picture, 'I'm sorry, with all the pain, I've caused you would think I'd remember it.'

Or block it from your memory said Jenna, no one blames you, we just want you back, even Millie, said Jenna and she misses you very much.'

'You have to come back with us' exclaimed Tyler.

Gregory suddenly gasped realising that he could lose Ben. Gregory was a little different from the other mice, he was chubby, and had one eye a little lop sided, he didn't quite fit in with the others, so Ben took him in just as he had done for Jake.

Ben looked at Gregory, 'but I can't right now he said, the mice need me, I can see that Gregory here will soon need another dose.' He held out his hand for Gregory to walk on to,' you've done very well my friend, Gregory looked pleased but weary, but you need rest now, it may take a week or two before this is over.'

'We understand said Jake but it would be too difficult to bring Millie here.'

'Perhaps it's best this way, said Jenna, it will give you and Millie both a chance to get used to this situation.'

'She's never going to believe this' said Tyler. Tyler's statement caused Ben to remember something.

'Here said Ben as he took a locket off around his neck to give to Jenna. Perhaps this will help. I was wearing it when they found me but I'm not sure what it is or how to open it.'

'It's Millie's locket said Jenna, she told me you gave it to her on your first wedding anniversary, and she insisted you wear it for good luck each time you went to look for our parents . . . she has the key that opens it . . . she wears it around her neck.'

'Hey yea said Tyler, that's right, now she'll have to believe us.'

Ben smiled trying to hide his nervousness about going back and he was grateful that the mice truly did need him. 'Well we should be going said Jake.'

'We'll be back soon' said Jenna. They both wanted to give Ben a hug but thought better of it. He would need time. Tyler on the other hand didn't give it another thought, ran up to Ben and gave him a big hug, Ben was grateful.

When they finally arrived home they found Millie in the kitchen cooking up another pot of stew. 'Oh I'm so glad to see you, I was beginning to worry, is everyone ok?'
'We're fine' said Jake.
'Guess who we met' said Tyler anxiously.
'Now just a minute said Jenna let Millie sit down.'
'Oh this sounds serious' said Millie with a bit of a laugh and a quick wink at Tyler as she took a seat.
'I'm afraid it is, said Jenna, o.k. Tyler you can tell her now.'
'We found Uncle Ben' he blurted out. Millie thought she wasn't hearing right and then she thought this was some kind of a terrible joke. She looked at Jake and Jenna and then back at Tyler who couldn't understand why she wasn't jumping for joy, and she realised it was the truth.
Trying to take this all in Millie was relieved that she was sitting. Trying to collect her thoughts, which felt as though they had been scattered by some terrible great wind, she finally found the worst one.
'Is he . . . is he . . . she couldn't bring herself to say the word dead.
'He's fine' said Jenna.
'He lives in the mountain with the mice' said Tyler, feeling as though he had to be excited for everyone. He's their teacher!
'He's the person Gregory was talking about' said Jake.
Gregory! Millie exclaimed as she just realised . . .
'That's right said Jenna, he named him after dad.'
'Millie was confused, 'but where is he, why didn't he . . .
'He's lost his memory said Jenna, he doesn't remember any of us, not even mom or dad.'

But you just said he remembered . . .

'He had a bad fall,' said Jake, he only remembered Gregory's name; Jenna had to tell him the whole story of how he got there.

'He didn't even know who he was said Tyler, Jenna had to tell him his name too.' Millie gave Jenna a sorrowful look, 'that must have been hard.'

'But he remembered Pleasantville, continued Tyler excitedly, he built a whole mouse village to look just like it.'

'That does sound like him' acknowledged Millie.

'It's him said Jake, he hasn't changed much.'

'He gave us this to give to you' said Jenna as she placed the locket into Millie's hand.

'Ben, she cried as she held the locket, why didn't he come back with you?'

'He wanted to Millie said Jenna but he couldn't leave the mice just yet, they're still too sick Millie looked back to the locket. 'Yes, of course,' she said.

'Ben wore it around his neck every day said Jenna, he thought it must have been important but he didn't know why.'

'Ben tried to open it said Jake.' Millie took the tiny key from around her neck and opened the locket. Inside, was a picture of her and Ben taken on their wedding day and the words, 'I'll love you forever, Ben. Millie closed her eyes and shed a few more tears. 'I must go to him she said.' 'I'm afraid you can't said Jake, the trek through the mountain is too dangerous.'

'Well then said Millie take this back to him, with the key.'

Jen nodded,' he said to thank you for the medicine, he really appreciated it, they have enough now for a couple more days.' Millie smiled and then she remembered the reason he went to the mountain. 'Did he say anything about your parents?'

'No, answered Jen, I'm afraid not,' we asked.

'Well said Millie I think I'll go to bed now, it was still early but that news had worn her out more than if she had made ten pots of stew. Everyone did the same, grateful that they found Ben and that the stew worked and that the next day would be Sunday and no one had to get up early.
Jake went back to his house and planned to sleep in but it was a while before he actually fell asleep; as he lie there thinking about Ben and all the events of the day, he was just so grateful to have Ben back; it felt as though he had received a wonderful gift.

# Chapter Six

## Reunions

Jake closed up his shop for the following week and told everyone he was doing his yearly inventory, but he was really making trips back and forth to Mouseville, with Millie's stew. On Jakes first trip back, he brought the locket with the key and a more recent picture of Millie, the nicest one she could find. She also sent a little note, though it took her most of the night to write it. She didn't know what to say, she didn't want to sound too anxious and scare him off, but she felt she had to say something. Millie knew she had to take this slow so all she wrote was . . . Dear Ben, I was glad to hear that you are alive and well; I hope the mice are doing better too; looking forward to seeing you . . . Take care, Millie. When Jake returned everyone, especially Millie was thrilled to see that Ben sent back a longer letter that read . . .

Dear Millie

I can't tell you how wonderful it was to finally see what was in the locket after all these years. Thankyou for sending it back with the key, and now I return it to you as it is yours. Thankyou also for the lovely picture you sent of yourself, you look very much like the picture in the locket, but I'm afraid I don't look quite like that anymore.

'Oh he's just being modest' said Jenna, he's just a little more gray that's all but he looks really good.

Millie wrote back thanking him for his kind words and sent more pictures of family members, his parents, brother, and some friends, she added a note describing who each one of them were. She thought it best to help him get his memory back before she'd say anything personal, so she kept her notes casual as though they were just friends. Jake brought him pictures of Pleasantville. Ben was astonished and perplexed at the same time.

'It's amazing he said, and yet a little disturbing.'

'What is' asked Jake?

'How is it said Ben that I can remember how to build a whole town stick for stick and yet I can't seem to remember the most important people in my life, I didn't even know my own name.'

Perhaps your mind decided that it was too painful to remember the loss of your brother' said Jake, it will come.

'I was grateful, said Gregory, from Ben's front pocket, (his favourite place), that you did remember Pleasantville because when I saw it, I thought for sure I'd find some help there.'

'It must have been quite a shock smiled Ben.'

'It was said Gregory, at first I thought I was going to find giant mice and I hoped they were friendly.' Ben and Jake laughed. Instead you found some good friends said Ben. Gregory nodded.


Ben knew Jake was doing all he could and was grateful for that. He picked up a picture of the both of them fishing.

'You seem like a very good friend, said Ben, I know Jenna said you were like a son but I don't know what she meant, are you my son?

'No' answered Jake.

'Oh good said Ben, Jake looked surprised, what I meant was I was afraid to hurt your feelings by not remembering you if you were my son.' Jake smiled.

'Do I have a son' Ben asked?

'No said Jake, you and Millie don't have any children.'

'So how did you and I meet asked Ben,' deciding it would feel awkward to ask anything about Millie, 'how did we become friends.'

Jake was hesitant to tell his story but he thought if it might help Ben to remember something he shouldn't hold back so he told him everything.

Ben was in shock 'I should have remembered that Ben said with a tear in his eye, I'm sorry Jake' he said as he gave Jake a hug. This wasn't the reaction Jake was expecting.

'Ah, it's ok said Jake patting him gently on the back, I have a great life now thanks to you and Millie.'

Poor Millie said Ben, taking a seat, how disappointed she must be.'

'No said Jake she understands. She can't wait to see you.'

'Well I don't think I'll be going back anytime soon.'

'You have to try' said Jake.

'It's not me said Ben it's the mice.'

'I thought they were getting better' said Jake.

'They seemed to, replied Ben and some of them, like Gregory here recovered completely, but many are still complaining of pain and dizziness even though they look much better, I just don't understand it.' Gregory was listening very intently to their conversation and walked over to where the pictures were. 'I don't know what the problem is' said Ben. 'I do' said Gregory. 'What??? asked Ben surprised.

'I know what the problem is' said Gregory.

'Really,???'

'Yes said Gregory, take me to the hospital room, and Jake, bring those pictures.'

'But its nap time said Ben, you should be napping too.'

'Trust me said Gregory, we won't wake anyone.'

Ben was confused but they went to the hospital room, no one saw them enter, they were all too busy . . . partying. Many of them were jumping up and down on their beds while some played out lively music on the bedposts and tiny little horns. There were even some swinging from the ceiling. Ben looked shocked and confused at the sight of it all as did Jake but none of the mice noticed them they were all too busy having a good time. Gregory hopped over to the shelf by the light switch and turned the light off and on and suddenly all the little mice ran for their beds and turned their little heads toward the door to wait for Ben to enter looking as sickly as possible. They soon realised that Ben and Jake had been there all along and they were caught.

'Oh whats the matter with you Gregory, said one of the mice, you're suppose to warn us before he comes in, not after!'

'Now just a minute' said Ben . . .

'It's ok said Gregory, listen everyone, I brought Ben and Jake here.' The little mice gasped.

'Hold these pictures up' he said to Ben and Jake. 'This is Ben's family, all the mice looked closely, they miss him very much said Gregory, they thought he was dead, but they're so glad he's alive and they want him back . . . and we don't have any right to keep him here.'

'My family worked very hard said Ben to make you well again I don't understand.'

'We don't want you to go away cried one little mouse, all the other mice chimed in agreeing, some crying.

Ben softened, 'I could never stay away from you he said, you are my family too, the only family I've known for the last five years, I can't just leave and never come back. I will find a way for us all to be together. Now has everyone recovered from the disease' Ben asked? Everyone nodded. 'Fine then said Ben, I will be back in five days, it won't be any longer than one of my trips up the mountain to the old cabin for leftover supplies.' That seemed to cheer some of them up. 'Whatever happens, I couldn't possibly live the rest of my life without you in it' assured Ben. That seemed to put them all at ease.

'We understand said Gregory doing his best to be brave, you go on we'll be all right.' Ben smiled at his little friend and patted his head. In five days he said.'

Soon Ben and Jake were on their way. Ben enjoyed the drive in Jakes truck. As they approached Pleasantville Ben was astounded by what he saw.

'I can't believe it, he said look at this, it's a giant mouse village, it's amazing.'

'What's amazing, said Jake, is that you remembered it all.'

'This really is my home' said Ben sounding surprised. Jake smiled as he pulled up in front of his place. 'You can stay here with me for now said Jake, till things get sorted.'

'Thank you' said Ben relieved as they got out of the truck, he didn't think he should just move in with his family. Ben followed Jake across the street. All of a sudden Ben stopped in his tracks.

'Ah, they're not expecting me, he said suddenly nervous 'perhaps you should go ahead and prepare them.'

'Na said Jake they've been prepared for you for some time.'

The front of the bakery was deserted as it was after hours but they heard some voices coming from the kitchen and went down the hall.

'Perhaps I should warn Millie' said Jake, a little worried about her reaction.

'Ill wait here' nodded Ben.

'Oh Jake your back' said Millie as he entered the kitchen. Jake could see she was struggling with a mixer. 'Need a hand,' he asked? Suddenly the mixer came on and flour went everywhere. 'Ah yelled Millie as she quickly turned it off, we'll fuss with that later she said, you must be hungry, how are the mice doing and how is Ben.' As Ben listened he thought she sounded like a very kind woman, her concern for the mice really touched him.

'The mice are fine said Jake.'

Jenna looked up from her paperwork.

'They are all better, they're cured, really,' asked Millie?

'Then Ben can come home' said Jenna.

'Actually said Jake, he' . . .

All of a sudden Tyler rushed in pulling Ben behind him. 'Hey look who I found.'

'Ben, said Jenna your here,' she ran and gave him a hug and led him to the table while poor Millie stood frozen on the spot looking red white and flustered.

Red because she was blushing, white because she had flour everywhere and flustered because she wasn't looking her best after a long day in the kitchen, nor was she wearing the pretty dress that she had picked out for the occasion, but grubby work clothes.

'As I was about to tell you, said Jake, he's here.'

Everyone looked at Millie; she didn't know what to say. Actually she had a few things she wanted to say to Jake, blaming him for the mess she was in but what she really wanted to do was to dig a hole and bury her self.

'I'm sorry said Jake, noticing her panicked look, that there wasn't much notice but . . . 'he went on to explain about the mice and their little scheme and how it was best they get out while they could before they hatch another plan to keep Ben there.

Millie was grateful for the lengthy explanation, it gave her a moment to get a grip and come back to her senses.

'I . . . I understand she said we're, ah certainly glad to have you here she continued and then she was at a loss for words.'

'Millie, said Jenna why don't you go and get cleaned up and I'll fix a meal for these boys.'

'Oh, good idea said Millie, if you'll excuse me,' she said as she made a hasty retreat to her room. When she saw what she looked like in the mirror she was horrified and didn't want to return to the kitchen.

'This didn't turn out quite the way she planned said Jenna as she set a plate of meat and potatoes in front of them but she'll come around, I'll just go and check on her.'

Tyler wanted to hear more about the party that the mice had as Jenna made her way upstairs. She found Millie cleaned up sitting on the edge of her bed in tears.

'Millie, are you ok?'

Millie looked up, 'it took everything to keep me from running out the back door, and I don't know why, but I don't think my legs have strength to carry me back down those stairs and back into that kitchen'

'I'll carry you if I have to,' teased Jenna, she noticed that Millie wasn't amused. 'Common Millie she said as she put an arm around her, we'll just take this one step at a time.'

Millie nodded and followed Jenna down stairs. Ben and Jake rose from their seats as they entered the kitchen.

'The food is lovely said Ben, thank you very much.' Millie nodded.

'Ben's going to be staying at my place for a while said Jake, so I can show him around, help him get used to things.' Millie found that she was so relieved to hear that, that she regained some of her strength. 'I'm sorry for all the trouble I've caused' said Ben.

'Nonsense said Millie you will come here for your meals every day just as Jake does and you are welcomed here any time.' Ben smiled and it lit up his face as Millie remembered it, she bit her lip to keep back the tears and gripped the chair in front of her to keep herself from running into his arms, or running out of the room as she tried to return his smile which is a little difficult when your biting the inside of your lip.

'Do you remember anything yet asked Tyler?' Ben silently shook his head no.

'Well it's been a long day said Jake, I think I should get Ben settled in.'

'Of course said Jenna, we'll see you for breakfast?
'Sure' said Jake with a smile as they headed for the door. Jake was feeling pretty good, with everything that happened lately, things between him and Jenna seemed back to normal.

The next morning Millie happily greeted them as though she had forgotten all about the night before and hoped they would too. The fact that she spent half an hour on her hair to get it perfect seemed to boost her confidence.
'Good morning she said, you look like you could use some breakfast, Ben and Jake were both stunned, it's waiting for you in the kitchen.' Millie decided that the best thing to do was to just be her self and treat Ben as a good friend. Ben and Jake were relieved to see her in a happy mood so they each decided to play along.
'The food is so wonderful said Ben, better than anything I've ever had in the mountain.'
'Well, said Millie, cooking was never your strong point.' Ben looked pleasantly surprised at how easily she went on about their past.
'But you were always good at building or fixing things, and fishing, you loved to fish, have you remembered anything?'
'No, I'm afraid not' he answered.
'Well, give it time' said Millie.
'I don't know said Ben, if I can't remember great food like this and great people like you it would seem there is little hope.'
'There is always hope' said Millie, a little blushed.
'Millie never gave up hope that we would see you again said Jenna' and here you are. There was a silent awkward moment but Millie went on, 'I thought we would have a little dinner party tonight with some of your old friends.'
'Oh don't go through any trouble' said Ben feeling as though she had already done too much.

'No trouble at all said Millie; you'll soon learn Ben, if you can't remember, that once I get a good idea in my head I go straight through with it.'

'That is a good idea Millie, said Jake; I'm going to take Ben around town today and were also going to see Doctor Harvey in Richville to see about his amnesia.' 'Ben and I remodled his house and he's anxious to see Ben.'

'Well that's a good idea too said Jenna but what did you say about Ben's absence for the past five years.'

'I told him he was lost in the mountains and had a bad fall, found an old deserted cabin and stayed there.'

'I guess that's pretty close to the truth said Jenna.'

'Can I come?' asked Tyler.

'Sure' said Jake.

Before long they were off and Millie and Jenna were busy with preparations for the dinner. Ben was amazed every time he saw a house or building he recognised but didn't remember. 'one thing puzzles me' he said.

What's that asked Jake?

'I didn't see a house that looks like mine back up in the mountain, was there one?'

'Yes replied Jake as he pulled up in front of large house, this used to be your property but after a year Millie sold it, and moved into the bakery, she was spending all of her time there anyways taking care of Tyler and Jenna and running the bakery. She used the money from the house to upgrade and furnish the bakery, it's more than doubled its income since then.

'She sounds like a very smart women' said Ben.

'She always was, said Jake, and these people tore down your small house and built this place.

Jake Ben and Tyler returned around four.

'What did the doctor say' asked Millie anxiously?

'He said it might take a little while' said Ben sadly.

'He also said, continued Jake that there may be something in Bens past that could trigger all of his memory to come back.'

'Well, said Millie cheerfully maybe tonight will unlock the past.'

By five thirty everything was set and Millie was in her pretty dress with her hair done up looking ten years younger. Guests started to arrive. The Clarks, Sarah and Peter were the first. Peter and Ben had been friends since high school so Millie thought he would be a good choice. Then the Fosters, Reg and Penny, who lived right next door to Ben and Millie till Ben disappeared and Millie moved into the bakery. And then there was Tom, James, Roger, and Frank all of who worked with Ben over the years and who were eager to help.

But Frank came more for Millie than he did for Ben. He had once tried to get her attention, years ago but she chose Ben instead and it was easy to see why. Frank was obnoxious. Always had to have his way and boasted about getting it. He had been trying to convince Millie to move away with him to the mainland ever since Ben's disappearance. Frank actually lived on the mainland but just happened to be visiting Roger for the weekend, though he didn't work with Ben for long, Millie invited him too not wanting to be rude, and she thought if there was a slight chance he could help Ben's memory . . .

She didn't appreciate the low whistle and sly wink Frank gave her as he entered but Millie tried not to let her disapproval show. Each guest brought with them old pictures and mementos they thought might spark a memory. Ben was thrilled to see it all and he enjoyed hearing about the old stories but he was also saddened because even after all this he couldn't remember a thing.

'Does any of this ring a bell' asked Tom?

'I'm afraid not' said Ben. He did how ever notice that Frank seemed to fancy Millie, every one seemed to notice that, the way he gave her winks, put his arm around her and even insisted on helping her carry things off to the kitchen, but Jenna said 'Millie you sit and enjoy your guests, Tyler Jake and I will clear this up.' Millie was relieved and appreciated the offer. She was tired of all Franks passes at her and certainly didn't want to be alone in the kitchen with him, but she felt that she had to be nice to him for Ben's sake. Even Roger was regretting that he had brought him, Ben wasn't quite sure what to make of it all, he only knew that all of Millie's efforts were not helping him and he felt bad for all the trouble she went through.

Jenna, Tyler and Jake brought out dessert as quickly as possible to get the evening over with, they realised that none of this was helping Ben and Frank was only making things worse. As soon as everyone was finished their dessert Roger stood making up some excuse for why they should leave. 'But it's still early' said Frank. Millie was grateful that her other guests caught on and also gave their excuses to leave. But Frank didn't seem to catch on 'Well I guess it's just me then.'

'Actually said Jenna the dinner is finished, we have a big day tomorrow, lots of orders to get ready, in fact we're going to be quite busy for the next few days' she said as she tossed him his jacket.

'Well perhaps I can come back to see Ben some other time.'

'If its Ben you want to see, he'll be at Jakes,' said Jenna as she slammed the door behind him and bolted it.

Millie was so embarrassed she was almost in tears, she quickly grabbed some dished and made off to the kitchen, but she had to quickly regain control because everyone wanted to help her. So did you remember anything Uncle Ben asked Tyler?

'Afraid not he replied sadly, I'm sorry you had to go through so much trouble for nothing Millie.'

'It wasn't any trouble' said Millie as she looked through the fridge for no reason, she just didn't want to face Ben. Then she spotted a large leftover pot of stew and pulled it out of the fridge. 'Jake this pot of stew is going to go to waste, why don't you and Ben take it to your place, in case you get hungry later on.'

'Sure' said Jake, willing to do anything she asked because he didn't quite know what to say about the evening, but Jenna could tell Millie just wanted to be alone, 'Millie you look tired, why don't you go to bed and we'll clean up this mess,' Millie looked unsure. 'I insist said Jenna, go and get some rest.'

'Alright alright, thankyou I'll see you all tomorrow.' They said goodnight and Jenna was glad Millie left because she wanted to talk to Ben, Millie was glad that Jenna was such a smart girl.

'So Ben what did you think about the whole evening, Jenna enquired.'

'Well, said Ben, it looks like I, ah have some good friends.'

'Yes you do said Jenna and a not so good friend, Ben looked puzzled, I mean Frank, he's not a friend at all.'

'He's not asked Ben?

No said Jenna, he just tagged along with Roger.'

'Well maybe, said Ben he's a friend of Millie's, he seems to be really taken with her and she seemed happy to'...

'She only seemed that way for your sake Ben, she didn't want to be rude' said Jenna.

'A lot can happen in five years,' said Ben.

'Not around here, Jenna quickly replied, trust me.' Jake had a feeling that might have been directed to him, and it was.

'You used to know Frank years ago and when Roger asked if he could bring him along Millie thought there could be a slight chance he might spark a long term memory or something. But she had been dreading it all day.' 'It took everything she had hold it together tonight.'

'She did seem a bit troubled' said Jake.

'Well you both know her better than I do,' said Ben.

'You should know this Ben, said Jenna, he asked her to marry him once, she chose you; she still does.'

Ben was silent for a moment. 'I can't imagine why he said sadly, he seems to be everything I'm not.'

'And that's why she chose you, because everything he is, is not good.' 'He`s been married three times Jenna added, but none of them could put up with him for long so don't think he has anything on you Ben, Millie`s a lot smarter than that, and if you think that after five years, you could feel anything for her' . . .

'I do said Ben, weather I get my memory back or not, there`s just something in me that tells me this is right.'

'I`m glad to hear that Jenna smiled, it`s a good place to start.'

'I can see why they made you a teacher,' smiled Ben.

Tyler, hoping Jenna wouldn't notice him, had been sitting at the table silent and as still as the pile of peas still on his plate, that never moved because he never ate them. He was usually sent to his room for such conversations.

But Tyler wasn't the only one listening in; upstairs Millie had gotten down on her knees to pray that God would somehow fix everything that went wrong tonight when she noticed voices coming through the vent on her floor. So she opened the vent wider, stayed on her knees and heard the whole conversation and knew that her prayers had been answered. Then she thanked God for sending Jenna to her and making her so smart.

Jake and Ben went to Jakes place. Jake brought the pot of stew to the kitchen and took down a couple of bowels from the shelf.

'I noticed you didn't eat much at Millie's,' he said.

'The food was good, it was great said Ben; it's just that I was . . . ah . . .'

'I understand said Jake as he warmed up some stew in a little pot on the stove, I often like a bowl of Millies stew before bed, he said, it helps me sleep better and you look like you could do with a good nights sleep.'

'I feel like I could too said Ben, but I did have a great day, thank you very much Jake.'

'No need to thank me said Jake, you're family.' Ben liked the sound of that, it made him feel like he finally belonged somewhere. As Ben took his first bite of stew he noticed a strange feeling come over him. 'What's wrong' asked Jake?

'Nothing said Ben, I just have a feeling that I've had his once before.'

'You have' said Jake, laughing. Ben was puzzled. 'What?'

'I've been carting this up to Mouse Ville for the past two weeks and you've never tried it?'

'No said Ben I thought it was medicine, I didn't know it was actual stew.'

'Well said Jake it was only the broth.'

'I suppose, said Ben that's why it seems familiar it was the smell of it.'

As Ben ate his stew he wished for a moment that he were back in the mountain helping his beloved mice instead of disappointing everyone here.

# Chapter Seven

## The Gathering

Ben lay down on the bed in the spare room Jake had set up for him, he felt exhausted and soon fell into a deep sleep. He dreamt first about the evening at Millies. He saw everything so clearly in his dreams. It felt good to see his friends again. He remembered way back when they were all in school together, even Frank who he never liked. How he pestered Millie, MILLIE! Yes he remembered Millie, how beautiful she was, and still is, how he loved her, and . . . yes, definitely still does. He remembered Jenna and Tyler and Jake. He was very proud of Jake, what a wonderful young man he had grown to be.

He remembered his brother, Gregory his only sibling and best friend, and Gregory's lovely, wife Shirley, and the terrible day of the avalanche. He then remembered searching and searching for them till he fell through the crack in the ice that led right into the mountain, and as he fell he yelled.

Then he felt someone shaking him and heard his name. He opened his eyes to see Jake there. 'Ben, are you alright he asked?

'JAKE! Ben exclaimed as he gave him a hug.' 'Oh Jake I'm so glad to see you.'

'Are you ok Ben, you were yelling?'

'Yes cried Ben, better, I remember, I remember everything.'

'You do?'

'Yes I remember Millie, the first time I saw her, oh wow he said as he looked off she wore a blue dress and looked like an angel.'

Jake smiled, Ben came back to the present a little embarrassed and quickly went on, I remember the old house we had, even the old cat, I remember teaching you how to hammer your first nail you hit your thumb you wanted to give up then and there.'

'That's right said Jake, and I'm glad you didn't let me.

'I remember your parents Jake, he sighed; you didn't deserve that but look at you now, such a fine young man.'

'I remember Jenna, how smart she always was, ah, did you and her ever ah . . .'

Jake nodded no.

'Oh said Ben, is there someone else then?'

Again Jake nodded no.

'Don't wanna miss your chances boy, look what I almost missed.'

'Tyler, he went on with a laugh; rascal.'

Ben's smile faded, and there was the pain, 'Gregory' he sighed.

Jake wasn't sure what to say. 'Are you o.k. Ben?'

Ben nodded, yea he sighed, 'I put Millie through enough; it's time to move on and I know just how I'm going to do it.'

'How' asked Jake, curious.

'Do you know what her favourite flower is' asked Ben?

'No' said Jake.

'Good said Ben because I do, and when she sees me arriving with lilies . . . do Sarah and Peter still have that flower shop around the corner.'

'Yes, cried Jake, you do remember everything, oh Millie's going to . . . well she might faint actually.'

'Yea she might said Ben, you be ready to catch her he laughed.'

Jake laughed too, 'well the sun's coming up now we'd better get ready, the flower shop won't be open yet but I'll give the Clark's a call and I know they'll have the lilies waiting for you.'

Jake was ready first. When Ben arrived downstairs Jake handed him an envelope. 'What's this he asked?'

'It's the money I owe you' said Jake. Ben looked in the envelope. 'My memory is back Jake, remember? You don't owe me anything.'

'I wouldn't be here if it wasn't for you, and if you have your memory back you should know that, and I want you to have this.'

'But there must be . . . hundreds.'

'A few said Jake, to start you off.'

'I don't know what to say' said Ben.

'That's easy replied Jake smiling, you just say how much for a dozen lilies.'

Ben laughed. It felt so good to hear Ben laugh, Jake almost felt like a young boy again.

The Clarks were so happy to hear about Ben that they gave him two dozen lilies on the house.


Meanwhile at the bakery Millie was beginning to wonder where Jake and Ben were.

'Oh they probably slept in said Jen.'

'That's not like Jake,' said Millie staring out the window.

'Yea, well they were probably up late talking' said Jenna as she looked out the side window. 'Maybe' said Millie still worried about the night before.

'Oh here they come now' said Tyler with a mouth full of sausage.

'Good morning boys, Millie said in her cheeriest voice, are you ready for breakfast?'

'I would like a big glass of water' said Ben in a joyful tone.

'Excuse me' asked Millie confused, he didn't sound like the same Ben of the last few days.

'For these' said Ben as he pulled out two dozen lilies from behind his back.

'Lilies, cried Millie, they're beautiful, Jake did you tell him?'

'Actually,' said Jake he told me, 'I didn't know.'

Millie froze, sudden silence filled the shop.

'That's right said Ben, I . . . remember, everything, Millie fell into the nearest chair, I remember the day we met, and you're still just as beautiful, I remember giving you that locket, all our years together, I remember, . . . searching the mountains, how you pleaded with me to stop, but I didn't listen and Im sorry Millie.'

Millie was feeling so many different emotions as she listened, gratitude, happiness, excitement even, but Ben's apology also released the hurt and anger she had bottled up for years and that emotion seemed to have won out as she abruptly got to her feet.

'Do you know that poor Jake looked for you for three weeks till I pleaded with him not to because I couldn't bear losing him too?' Ben looked at Jake in sorrow. 'At least he listened to me, it was unbearable enough losing Gregory and Shirley, then you . . . did you really think a feeble apology and two dozen lilies could fix that, do you have any idea of the hell we went through!!?!'

Millie realised by the look on everyone's face that they were all in shock by her outburst and she seemed to calm down some, 'but it's been five years I guess I should have forgiven you by now, I'll get some water for these she said as she grabbed the flowers and went to the kitchen.'

She needed an excuse to leave as she was about to burst into tears. No one moved or barely breathed as she walked out.

'Well that went well' remarked Jenna with a smirk on her face.'

'Not as well as I hoped said Ben.'

'Do you remember that she never holds a grudge for long said Jenna?'

'It has been five years; I guess she has a lot to grudge about affirmed Ben

'Well said Jenna as she gave him a hug, I'm happy for you, I'm sure Millie is too.' 'She didn't plan on being angry when your memory returned, it just came out that way; she has bottled up a lot of pain.'

Just then Millie came scurrying back from the kitchen.

'Millie, I'm so sorry pleaded Ben I . . .'

'We'll discuss that later Millie cut in, right now we have a little emergency.'

She opened her hands and there lay Gregory all out of breath.

'Gregory" exclaimed Ben, what happened!' But Gregory couldn't talk.

'I'll get him some stew' said Jenna as they all rushed to the kitchen.

'I hope this works said Millie.'

'You know, it was your stew that brought Bens memory back' said Jake as Jenna poured a little of it in a bowel.

'Oh, really,' said Millie.

'Yes said Jake, we had some last night, before bed, and in his dreams everything returned.'

'Ben, said Jenna that's amazing, isn't it Millie!'

Millie didn't know what to say but she didn't have to worry about it because after a few sips of the stew, suddenly Gregory was able to stand. 'It's the weasels Teacher, they're back, one was after me, I lost him in the tunnels.'

'It wasn't Duchess that kept them away Teacher, they know you've left the mountain.'

'Duchess, weasels' asked Millie?

'Duchess is a three legged cat,' explained Tyler, she lost her leg in a fight with the weasels, then Ben showed up and they haven't been back since.

'I didn't even stop to think about the weasels said Ben, they never bothered the mice when I hiked to the camp for a few days.

'They've grown, said Gregory and, they look different, it looked as if there were about hundred of them.'

'How did you get away' asked Jenna? 'Are there anymore here' she said looking around.

Gregory was silent for a moment. 'I . . . I, was already in the tunnel when they attacked. I was . . . coming to see you Ben, then I heard . . . screaming, I ran back and peeked, it was terrible, one spotted me, I ran,' he cried.

'There was nothing you could do said Ben, you did the right thing.'

'I feel like I deserted everyone said Gregory, and though you haven't been gone long, I missed you, and I wanted to see if you got your memory back and if, if, you're going to stay here.'

Ben looked around at everyone and his eyes landed on Millie, 'I don't know what I'm doing yet, but right now we have to get back there.'

'We'll come too' said Jenna.'

'I have a few hunting rifles at the store' said Jake.

'I can shoot said Tyler excitedly!'

'No! came the answer from Jenna Millie and Jake all at once, and if you give us a hard time about it you can stay here said Jenna!' That quieted Tyler's protest. 'Now hurry and get ready.'

Tyler hurried to get ready as did everyone else. Soon they were all on their way. Jake brought the rifles, one for him and Ben, and flashlights for everyone, Jenna brought a large knapsack to carry mice in and a jar of Millie's stew for emergencies. And Tyler brought his slingshot and baseball bat, two weapons he knew he could get away with.

'Why did you bring the flashlights asked Tyler, there's lots of light in there,' he said as they approached the entrance. 'Hey where's the light???'

'Shh' said Jenna. Ben had let Gregory down to turn on the lights. 'It's not working' he said.

'Just as I thought' said Ben, these weasels can see in the dark.' Everyone turned their flashlights on and they walked on towards Mouseville, it was difficult enough in the light but in the dark it was hazardous.

Finally as they approached the tiny village they were shocked by the sight that lay before them. The little mouse village was in ruins, demolished by the weasels. Poor Ben was horrified at the sight. 'Oh no he cried what have I done?'

'This isn't your fault Ben,' said Jenna.

'Yes, yes it is; I should never have left.'

'We'll find them' said Jake determined. Gregory was silent but he was feeling just as guilty as Ben. They walked on to Ben's house and found it still standing, but inside was a shambles. There's a trap door over here, said Ben, that leads to a hidden passage underground, mice could be there, they have their own entrance outside. Everyone was hopeful as they entered the underground passage, they searched and they called but found no one. Ben sat down on a boulder and sighed in despair, I guess they didn't make it to the house he sighed.'

'There's another place declared Gregory a little hopeful, it's the children's hide out that none of the parents know about, but they showed it to me, they like me, made me promise not to tell,'he added, feeling guilty thinking that if he had told the parents maybe some of them could have been saved. 'It's this way' he said as he scurried off.

In a few short minutes they arrived at a little knoll. This is it he said. Where said Tyler, all I see is a little hill. Exactly said Gregory as he picked up a stick and poked it at a precise spot in the ground. To their amazement a little door flipped open. Tyler was so anxious to see inside that he dropped to the ground to take a look and popped back up just as fast with mud splattered on his face. It's the weasels he cried. I doubt that laughed Gregory, weasels would sooner take a bite out of you than throw mud at you. Jenna would have laughed at the sight of Tyler too if they weren't so worried about the mice. Gregory stood at the entrance 'its ok he called, you can come out; Teacher is back. Several little mice scurried out jumping all over Gregory.

Oh thank goodness cried Jenna.'

'Gregory, we knew you'd come for us said one,' 'We knew you would save us cried another.'

Gregory was shocked; he thought they would all be excited to see Teacher.

He looked up at Ben a little embarrassed; Ben got down on his knees, grateful to see the little ones but still worried about the others. One of them had brought their Grandfather with them

'The strongest ones led the weasels through the tunnel to Richville, he said. 'Won't the folks in Richville be surprised' laughed Tyler.

'Yea said Jenna as the mice climbed into her knapsack, almost as surprised as you were,' she added, wiping a little mud off his face.

'Oh was that you said one of the older mice, Tyler smiled, I'm sorry.'

'It's ok said Tyler I'm just glad you were all right.' 'Do you think the others will be ok, and why Richville?'

'I'm sure they will' claimed the Grandfather mouse.

'That tunnel quickly narrows so that so that only the mice can get through.'

Jenna carefully put the knapsack on her back and the little mice poked their heads out of its many pockets. Everyone was grateful to not have found any little bodies on their way to the tunnel entrance but as they approached the entrance they saw something lying on the ground.

'Oh no' cried Ben as he knelt and petted the long white fur of Dutches's coat.

'I have some stew said Jenna, perhaps . . .'

'It's too late said Ben.' He took off his jacket and wrapped it around the cat as he picked it up. 'I'm not leaving her here for the weasels.'

'I'm sorry Ben' said Jenna as Jake flashed his light into the tunnel. 'It looks like it's clear in there,' he said.

'They must have got away' encouraged Tyler.

'Duchess must have held them off till she could fight no longer' said Ben. No one knew what to say.

'They'll head for Millies he continued we should get back.'

As they walked Tyler thought he saw something and suddenly stopped.

'What is it' asked Jenna who bumped into him?

'I saw something move, over there, are there any more mice, or do you think it could be . . .'

Just then a pack of ferocious looking weasels charged towards them. Jake shot at them and they ran off.

'It's not like weasels to attack humans like that' declared Ben.

'Do you suppose the disease is affecting them too' asked Jenna?

'It's very possible' said Ben, we'd better hurry.'

So off they went climbing higher and higher along the narrow cliff that seemed to get even narrower with every few steps. Suddenly, from a ledge above them leaped ten weasels landing upon Jake. He dropped his rifle and it landed near Tyler, as he fought to get them off. Ben and Tyler turned to help him but it all happened so quickly, they attacked Jakes legs and he fell taking most of the weasels with him. Jenna and Ben watched in horror as they were quite far up, 'JAKE!!!' yelled Tyler, they called his name a few times but their only answer was horrible squeals from the weasels.

'We have to go after him,' he cried!'

'We won't stand a chance' said Ben as Jenna held Tyler back.

'But they'll eat him' cried Tyler.

'No they won't, declared Ben, they're not after us they're after the mice.'

'We have to do something groaned Tyler we can't just leave him.'

'We don't want to leave him either said Jenna, but . . .'

'We'll have to get help said Ben, common the sooner we go the sooner we can get back.'

Tyler remained frozen in place, he couldn't bear the thought of leaving Jake behind.

'We've got the mice, said Jenna, they'll be back and if we don't get out of here soon we might not get out at all. We won't be much help to Jake then.'

Tyler reluctantly gave in and turned to follow them. Just then he saw something move out of the corner of his eye, Tyler grabbed Jakes rifle and shot the two remaining weasels as they were about to pounce on Jenna.

He held out the gun for one of them to take it.

'Thank you, you keep it' said Jenna, Tyler was surprised, 'you obviously know how to use it.'

'That was some pretty amazing shooting' said Ben.

This made Tyler feel a little better at least he felt like he was doing something.

'Besides said Ben with all the noise we made I'll bet the whole gang will be up here soon.'

'Let em come' replied Tyler as they walked on.

They were finally near the top when Jenna thought she heard something. 'Stop' she said, Ben and Tyler froze, I hear something.' 'I hear it too' said Tyler. 'They're close said Ben we must hurry!' They rushed on as fast as they could on that steep ledge and almost made it to the opening when Tyler let out a yell. A weasel had latched on to his leg, Jenna swung her foot, kicked it and it went flying off the ledge, squealing all the way. This made the rest of them move in even faster.'

'Run!!!,' yelled Ben, Jenna hurried as fast as she could, with her sack of mice and a dead cat in her arms, as Tyler and Ben shot at the massive pack of weasels behind them.

They made it to the opening, Jenna climbed through, then Tyler, who immediately noticed that Ben was still in the cave, about to be attacked. He wanted to shoot but Ben was in the way. He looked up and saw lots of stalacktites hanging from the ceiling looked at the large number of weasels and got an idea. While Ben was firing at the weasels, holding them back, Tyler started firing at the stalactites directly above the weasels. 'What are you doing' demanded Jenna? But Tyler was too busy to answer. 'Run!!!' He yelled to Ben. Ben made it out just in time as much of the ceiling fell on the weasels. He was scratched, and bleeding but grateful to be out.

'Smart thinking boy' he said to Tyler.

Tyler would have been excited and delighted if he wasn't so worried about Jake.

'That was brilliant, claimed Ben; I didn't think I was going to make it out.'

'I hope Jake makes it out said Tyler'I hope those rocks didn't land on him,' he replied as he started down the mountain wiping a tear away.

If Jakes as smart as you I'm sure he'll be fine,' replied Ben trying to calm him.

They hurried down the mountain as fast as they could. It was getting dark and they worried more about Jake with each step, then suddenly they heard a loud horn.

'Jake!!!' yelled Tyler as they rushed toward the repeating sound of the horn.

Though he had a broken arm, a large gash in his leg and some bruised ribs, which was all very painful, Jake was able to drag himself along. The weasels left him for dead and went after the others. Jake kept blowing the horn and was about to try and drive somewhere else when he heard the faint call of his name so he blew the horn till he saw them.

The horn also alerted the few weasels that were left in the mountain; they too headed for the truck. Luckily Tyler saw them as they got near the truck and shot the three of them.
'Nice shooting' said Jake as he looked from the weasels to them.
'Jake you made it' said Ben, so relieved.
'You're ok' cried Tyler happily giving him a hug.
'Well I think my arm is broken' he replied.
'How did you get out,' asked Jenna.'
I saw some more weasels coming up out of a large hole in the ground near where I landed, I thought since they didn't live in the mountain, the hole must lead outside. After they were gone I climbed through it. 'It was a tight squeeze in some spots but I was surprised at how big it was, they must come through in bunches.
Jenna, was also relieved to see Jake, she didn't think he would have survived the fall or the weasels. I'll drive, she said, we'd better get out of here before any more of these show up,' she said looking at the dead weasels. They look kind of strange don't they?'
'It's the disease said Ben as he climbed into the truck. I expect it will kill the rest of them off soon.'

Millie was so relieved to see them all back safe and sound; she kept wiping a tear from her eyes trying hard not to make a big fuss. 'What happened,' she asked?

Tyler started in and everyone let him tell his story, Millie was a little shocked to see that everyone was agreeing with him. 'Oh my soul, she said it's a miracle you all made it back here in one piece it's no wonder you all look such a frightful mess, oh but I almost forgot, you're not the only ones to have made it back.' They followed her into a small room by the pantry, and on the floor, on a nice soft blanket lay the rest of the mice, sleeping, and in the corner sat a few small bowels of Millie's stew. A few of the mice had woken.

'Teacher is that you, are the children . . .'

'We have them said Ben, falling to his knees, being overcome with emotion, they're ok.'

Jenna set the back pack she was carrying on the floor, hoping Ben was right, the way they got bounced around in there, but the tired little mice ran to their parents for anxious embraces. The mice were filled with gratitude thanking Ben and the others over and over.

'You can thank Gregory, said Ben, he risked his life to come get us and led us to them.' Ben didn't have the heart to tell them about Duchess, and how bravely she died to protect them.

Gregory looked at Ben, grateful for his words but wondered, 'what will happen to us now?'

'I don't know replied Ben, but you won't be going back there, we'll figure something out, just get some rest for now.' Gregory hopped onto the soft blanket exhausted and went right to sleep.

'I should get you to the hospital' said Jenna to Jake once the door to the mice room was closed. 'Millie worried, 'Hospital???'

'Jake broke his arm,' Jenna answered.

'I'll take him said Ben, you get some rest.'
'Are you sure' asked Jenna?
'Yea said Ben, we'll be fine besides in a few hours it will be time to feed the mice again and Millie might need some help.'
'All right then said Jenna,' we'll see you in the morning.

Ben didn't want to stay behind with Millie because he wasn't quite sure she had forgiven him yet. Everyone was grateful that the next day was Sunday because they could sleep in. The doctor believed Jakes story of tripping over tools in the dark and told him to be more careful.

# Chapter Eight

## The New Secret Keeper

After breakfast the next morning, everyone went in to see the mice Gregory had already explained to them about Duchess, they were sad to hear the news but they thought, like Millie, that it was a miracle everyone else made it back. Ben dug a grave in Jakes back yard for Duchess and laid her to rest, and although Millie said the mice were welcome to stay Ben knew they couldn't spend the rest of their lives in a room. The rest of the day went by rather quietly, everyone trying to come up with new ideas for the mice, but not having much luck.

Ben couldn't sleep much that night. Jake woke the next morning to find him busy in the back workshop; he was making little houses for the mice.

'Wow Ben, he said, look at these, you must have been up all night.'

'I couldn't sleep, I'll pay you for the wood' said Ben.

'Naw said Jake that's only scrap I'm glad to see it being put to good use. Did you figure out a plan?'

'No said Ben but I had to do something.'

'One step at a time said Jake.'

'One step at a time, repeated Ben, that's what Millie used to say.'

'She still does' smiled Jake. 'Why don't you get some rest I'll continue on here.'

'I don't know' said Ben.

'Well I know, if Millie saw you looking so tired she would never forgive me for letting you do all this work on your own.'

'Alright said Ben I'll go but don't let me sleep too long.'
Jake nodded but thought, 'only as long as you need to.'

Jake decided to keep the shop closed for a few days using his broken arm as an excuse but he actually just wanted time to try and help figure things out. He was grateful that it was his left arm that was broken because he found he could still do quite a bit with just his right hand and he could hold things in place with his broken one, so he got to work.

Soon there came a knock at the door, it was Millie and Jenna with baskets of food. Jake was surprised to see them. Tyler stayed behind with the mice.
'Is it breakfast time already' Jake asked?
'We're a little early said Millie but we wanted to see how you boys were doing.'
Jake smiled as he let them in, 'come see what Ben did.'
He led them into the workshop where they saw several tiny little houses.
'Oh my,' said Millie, sounding a little concerned, he must have been up all night.
'I didn't know said Jake, guess those pain pills the doctor gave me really knocked me out, but I just sent him to bed.'
'He's rebuilding Mouseville said Jenna, what's he going to do with them?'
'He's not sure yet but he feels he has to do something' answered Jake.
'This looks like your toolbarn said Millie holding up one of the houses and here's the bakery.' 'Why don't we paint them for him said Jenna, it would be a nice surprise.'
'Great idea, agreed Jake, I'll get some paint.' In a few moments he returned with a box of paint supplies.

Before long three of the houses were finished, the Tool Barn, the Bakery and the Town Hall, just in time because Ben came back down stairs. Tears welled up in his eyes as he saw the houses, and he was speechless.

'Ben, are you o.k.' asked Jenna? He shook his head yes. 'Is this o.k. Ben she continued, if you don't like the paint we can . . .' Ben looked at her in exasperation, 'it's wonderful he managed to say, and I don't deserve such wonderful friends,' excuse me he said as he left the room to blow his nose.' He returned a few minutes later to three very worried people and took a deep breath. 'I'm sorry, about that, I . . .'

'Nonsense said Millie, you've been under a lot of pressure lately and none of it was your fault, and . . . I'm sorry I wasn't more understanding,' she added thinking about the day before.

'You had your own pressures Millie,' said Ben with a warm smile, and I'm sorry too.'

And that seemed to settle all the upset of the past five years. Everyone seemed to breath a deep sigh of relief.

The rest of the day was spent working on the houses with Millie and Ben complimenting each other every chance they had. Jenna and Jake both found it cute. Everyone was in much better spirits by the time Tyler had the mice down for their nap and came over to see what was happening and what was for dinner. He was amazed by what he saw. 'Wow these look even better than the old ones, what are you going to do with them all, where are you going to put them?'

'One step at a time said Ben, one step at a time.'

'That's what Millie always says' declared Tyler, everyone smiled, Millie blushed a little.

Ben checked on his mice before supper, they were sleeping again. 'Are they ok asked Millie, do they usually sleep this much?'

'Not usually but they're still probably tired from yesterday' answered Ben.

After supper they went to the town hall for the annual Christmas production meeting. It was opened to everyone but aside from the members of the town hall committee, who came more out of obligation than anything else, there were few others who came. Tyler stayed with the mice; he enjoyed spending most of his time with them, especially Gregory.

Mayor McGregor welcomed everyone and was clearly disappointed that more didn't show up, he wasn't the only one disappointed, the Mayors son Matt was also there hoping to see his best friend Tyler, who always followed Jake everywhere and since Jake was there he thought Tyler might be too.

Matt had come to see Tyler the day before and Millie told him he was gone hunting with Jake, it was the best story she could come up with on the spur of the moment.

This upset Matt because they always invited Matt along on trips. Although they never went hunting before, Matt felt a little put out that he wasn't invited too. Tyler never even mentioned a hunting trip he thought, he must have been keeping it a secret, they never kept secrets, maybe Tyler didn't want to be friends anymore, and today he couldn't reach any of them. He went to the bakery after lunch; Tyler had already gone to Jakes. Jake had a closed sign on his door so Matt assumed he was still hunting or gone on one of his deliveries.

Mayor McGregor had listed the plans that the town hall came up with for decorations and activities, everything was pretty much the same as last year, give the decorations a new coat of paint, and have a pot luck dinner and dance, oh and send to the mainland for new lights, the old ones kept burning out last year. Then he invited everyone to share their ideas. A few people mentioned they had some old ornaments they could donate. 'Why bother,' said Willard Stott, a disgruntled man, 'we can never outshine Richville or even Midville.' Everyone knew that Willard's sole purpose for showing up to these town meetings was to complain.

'We don't have to' said Mrs Noles, secretary to the Mayer, 'this year the judging will be on uniqueness.'

'Uniqueness?!!!? replied Willard 'what's that suppose to mean.'

'It means different! Original! Like you Willard,' she shot back with a sarcastic smile. Willard didn't quite understand the meaning of her reply but since her remark drew a few laughs from the audience, he was not impressed but remained silent.

Mayor McGregor really appreciated his secretary at times like this. Many believed she not only wore the pants in her home, married to Earl, an easy going fella who worked at the post office, but many also said she wore the pants in the office as well. It was no wonder Mayor McGregor and Earl were good friends. Both their wives were similar. Mrs McGregor refused to cancel her bridge game to go to the meeting and she didn't care what the town or her husband had to say about it either.

Since no one had any ideas the Mayor was just as happy as everyone else to end the meeting. 'The sign up, sheet is still at the entrance for anyone wanting to sign up for the Christmas tree committee' he said, 'I thank you all for coming.'

The Mayor left by the back door avoiding Willard. People who came to the meeting hoping to get a little Christmas spirit left feeling even more depressed than when they had arrived.

Though the Mayor was doing the best he could to take care of his little town, quite a few fishing boats were either damaged or destroyed in that storm on Halloween night even though most of them were tied up. Answering the peoples cries for assistance to get them back on their feet left little money in the budget for parties and such, though the people didn't seem to care as much about answering the Mayor's cries for assistance. The only names he would find on the signup sheet under Jakes, was Bens, Millie's and Jenna's.

Needless to say Matt never heard a word of the meeting but as soon as it was over he asked Jenna about Tyler. Jenna, not knowing about Millie's little story, told Matt that Tyler had been sick the past couple of days. Matt wanted to protest, but he went hunting yesterday, but he quietly walked away thinking the whole family was against him

The next day Tyler said he wasn't feeling well and asked if he could stay home from school. Jenna had a sneaky suspicion that he just wanted to stay with the mice but since he was doing pretty well at school and with Tyler tending to the mice, she felt that this would free up more time for Ben and Millie to be together, so she agreed, 'but only for one day.' Jenna wished she could stay home too as she went off to work. She thought of how Ben and Millie seem to be growing closer every day even though Ben was still living at Jakes place, he said Jake needed his help, which he sometimes did with his arm still in a cast, but everyone knew he just wanted to take things slow. Millie gave him the time and space he needed but secretly wished he'd move along a little faster.

Ben and Jake ate leftovers at Jakes that night so they could spend more time working on the houses.

After supper Tyler was of course, feeling better and he along with Jenna and Millie went to Jakes to continue their work.

Gregory came along in Tyler's shirt pocket as he became accustomed to doing but this was the first time he road along to Jakes place.

'Wow' he said once he had seen the houses.

Ben was surprised to see Gregory there but pleased, 'do you like them?'

'Oh yes I do very much, the others will be so surprised. But where are we going to put them?'

'I don't know said Ben, one, step at a time' everyone else smiled. Gregory wondered what was so funny.

Just then they heard a knock at the back door, more like a pounding.

'Hey let me in demanded a voice, I know you're in there Tyler.'

'It's Matt said Tyler with eyes big and round, what do we do.'

'Is he your friend' asked Ben?

'Best friend' said Tyler.

'I NEED TO TALK TO YOU!!!' The voice and the pounding grew louder.

'In that case we'd best let him in said Ben with a smile, friends are important.'

'NOW!!!' Yelled Matt as the door swung open. Matt was embarrassed to see everyone standing there.

'What's going on' he demanded?

'What do you mean' asked Tyler?

'What do I mean?!!! You're never around! You're always busy! You even went hunting! [everyone but Millie was puzzled] Today you missed school, and you don't look sick.'

Matt gave Jenna a scowl and Tyler guessed he asked about him and that Jenna must have said he was sick, but he had no clue about the hunting accusation.

'I have been a bit busy' said Tyler.

'A bit??!!! What's so important!!!??' Tyler looked at Ben and Jake for help. 'Matt, Tyler says you're his best friend' said Ben. 'Well I thought so' answered Matt.

'Well since you're his best friend perhaps we could trust you with a secret, probably the biggest secret you'll ever be asked to keep.' Matt's eyes were almost as wide as his mouth but he managed to nod yes.

'Well you look like you can be trusted smiled Ben come this way.' Ben led him to where all the finished houses were lined up and for the first time they didn't get such a great reception.

'This is the big secret, said Matt to Tyler, your building a bunch of bird houses.' 'They're not bird houses said Tyler.'

'Then what???!' Tyler looked at Ben who nodded.

'They're for mice he answered.

'Mice??? That's crazy' declared Matt.

'And what's so crazy about that' piped up a little voice from inside Tyler's pocket.

'Who said that' asked Matt looking around.

'You're hearing voices asked Gregory, who's crazy now?' Ben and the others laughed a little, Tyler didn't know what to think, he was afraid he might loose his best friend if he didn't know the truth soon and then he was afraid he might loose his his best friend if he did know the truth. 'Alright Gregory said Ben I think it's time you meet a new friend.'

Matt thought it was strange for Tyler's uncle to be calling him Gregory, as he was looking right at Tyler. And then he saw a little head poke out of Tyler's pocket. 'What's that???!' Tyler set Gregory on the counter,

'This is Gregory' answered Tyler. Matt looked at him strangely.

'Haven't you ever seen a mouse before' asked Gregory? 'Ahh' yelled Matt as he jumped back. 'He looks like he's just seen a ghost said Gregory, not a mouse.'

'I . . . I . . . never saw one that talks, said Matt; poking Gregory, where's the switch, did you get this from, the mainland?'

'I'll give you a switch if you don't stop that' scolded Gregory.

Matt jumped back again but he wasn't scared this time, still believing Gregory was a toy, 'hey that's pretty neat,' he declared. Gregory became frustrated, 'Oh I give up,' he said as he turned and walked to Ben.

'Just give him a minute' said Ben.

'I think it will take a lot more than a minute to get through his thick . . .'

'Gregory! Scolded Ben, is that how we treat a guest?'

'No said Gregory I guess not, I'm sorry.' Ben motioned for him to appologise to Matt, which he did. Matt stood stunned as the reality of everything he was seeing washed over him like a scary movie. His heart was pounding faster as he looked to Tyler and wanted to say, good one Ty, Ill get you back.

'Are you o.k. Matt' asked Tyler as Jake got him a chair.

Tyler explained everything from the beginning while the others got back to work on the mouse's houses. 'WOW' was all Matt could say over and over again. Tyler especially liked telling about the part where he got to use the gun and how well he did. Matt looked at the others and their expressions confirmed Tylers words. 'Wow' . . . was all Matt could say. Ben got an idea. 'Tyler, why don't you and Gregory take Matt to your place and you and the others can explain . . .'

'Others' asked Matt?

'Common said Tyler, we'll show you.' Matt followed Tyler out the door and the others got back to work. Millie decided to give the houses a Christmas theme by painting little wreaths and other Christmas decorations on it.

Tyler, Matt and Gregory returned about an hour later.
Ben was anxious to ask, 'so what do you think?'
'Amazing' said Matt exited.
'You know you can't tell anyone' said Ben.
'Of course said Matt, who would believe me anyway he said as he took another look at the houses.
'These houses are really coming along he said, feeling like he belonged to a very special club, they look like the little Christmas houses we have at home, Mom puts them in the tree.' Jenna, Millie Jake and Ben all looked at each other, and froze with paint brushes and hammers in mid air.
'Did I say something wrong asked Matt?'
'Of course,' said Jenna!
'I did???
It would certainly comply with the requirements for something different, unique,' she went on, ignoring poor Matt, who was getting worried.
'It would' agreed Jake.
'What are you talking about' demanded Tyler?
'The tree in the town square' said Millie happily.
'The mice can't live the rest of their lives in your house said Ben.'
'But what about cats' asked Tyler worried. Ben, Millie, and Jenna all looked at each other looking for an answer but then altogether said one step at a time. Jake laughed a little, we'll figure it out he said.
As they carried on their work Matt continued, 'this year Mom bought some big angel statues and a manger set for the front yard. I saw her hiding it from dad cause she's probably scared he'll make her take it back. I heard him say when she said she wanted it, that it wouldn't look too good

to have such a big display in our front yard when so many people are having such a hard time and some won't even get a Christmas this year. I'm afraid we're not going to get a Christmas this year when he finds out that she hid it till Christmas eve so he couldn't make her take back, he's going to be boiling mad. Mom usually gets her way but when he's had enough, watch out. She only bought it cause it was bigger than Aunt Martha's set in Midville.'

After a couple more hours of work they decided to bring the finished houses over to surprise the mice and they loved them, they were so surprised and much more hopeful about their futures. The thrilled little mice just couldn't wait to move in. Not all the houses were finished yet so they shared but Gregory got left out. Because he was a little different none of the other mice were really close to him. Gregory didn't mind actually because he liked staying in Tyler's room. Tyler was a better friend to him than any of the mice were, well except for the children.

Jenna noticed that the mice in some of the storey books at school were wearing clothes which gave her a great idea, so she decided in her spare time, of which she had very little, between exam marking and Christmas baking, that she would make some new Christmas clothes for them to surprise them for Christmas, it was a busy time for everyone.

Millie was busy baking and painting, Tyler and Matt were busy with exams and helping out at the tool barn, and with the mice. Matt kept his word as promised and spent most of his time over at Tylers. His parents didn't mind because they had their own Christmas preparations to worry about. The Mayer put Jake and Ben in charge of the Christmas tree dilemma because they were the only ones who had any idea about what to do with the tree and he liked the little house they had brought with them to show him. He was also happy that his son Matt was helping out for two reasons, it kept Matt out of trouble and made himself look good.

## Chapter Nine

—*◊◊◊*—

# Lights????

One evening Ben and Jake brought over all the old Christmas ornaments stored in the town hall. Some of it could be used but most of it was just plain worn out, and Jake feared that if they had to use the old, patched up set of tree lights that they might just set what was left of the poor old tree, on fire, so that Saturday they planned a trip to the mainland for new lights. Tyler was especially excited, he and Matt were invited to tag along and he had never been to the mainland in his life. Matt had been there a few times but this time was special because he got to go with his best friend instead of being dragged behind his mother and sister like on his last trip.

On the morning of the big day, the boys got up extra early to get their chores done so they could make it to the ferry by 9:00 a.m. Tyler couldn't believe his eyes when he saw the size of the main land city before him. He never saw buildings so tall or crowds so big. It was a bit frightening really but he saw so many new and wonderful things he had never seen before and one was a bicycle that he swore would be etched in his memory till the day he died. It was the latest model and no one on the island had anything like it.

Yes they saw many great things but the one thing that seemed to be in short supply of everywhere they went, was out door Christmas tree lights. 'Oh we just sent out a large order to Richville' they were told, or 'someone from Midville was here yesterday and bought the lot.' It seemed they had sold more lights to Richville and Midville combined than they did to the people on the mainland.

The mainland cities had their own competitions as well but many people from the mainland greatly enjoyed going to the island every year for the compition. This pleased the Governor very much because not only was he Governor of the mainland, but he was also Governor of the island and wanted to promote support for the island.

On their way home Tyler and Matt were still excited over everything they had seen that day. Ben and Jake though were a little concerned over their lack of tree lights, they had returned on the latest possible ferry so they could have more time searching. Millie and Jenna decided that they were so late because they had so many lights to carry and were a little dissapointed when they saw how little there actually was, though they tried hard not to show it.
'Perhaps they'll get more in later' said Jenna trying to sound hopeful for Ben's sake.
'Lots of places have more on order but it will be too late for us said Jake, we have to start decorating next week he added.'
'This won't cover the whole tree' said Jenna, looking hopelessly at their meagre decorations.
'I know replied Jake; we'll put the lights on last and hope someone will come up with some more in the mean time.'
'One step at a time said Millie,' everyone looked at her a little doubtful; it's worked so far she added, we'll just all pray for lights tonight.' 'Now common to the kitchen, I've got your supper ready.'
The atmosphere was quiet around the table when Gregory came in. 'Your back' he said happily as he scurried up to the kitchen table.
'Hey, said Tyler, how you doing?'
'Great now that your back' said Gregory. 'It's been kind of boring here without you, did you have a good day?'
'It was awesome' said Tyler. 'Yea really' agreed Matt.

'Oh you should have been there said Tyler, they had lots of toy stores and so many things I've never seen, tall buildings and busses that take people around, and so many cars everywhere, I'm glad you weren't there Gregory, I almost got run over but Matt pulled me back just in time.'

'Ya gotta watch the traffic lights said Matt, my sister took her puppy to the city once, what she did that for I don't know but he didn't make it back, big bus got him.'

Gregory gulped and decided that mainland was definitely not a place for him. 'So did you get lots of decorations he asked anxious to change the subject?'

'Not really said Tyler, Richville and Midville bought all the lights.'

'What lights' asked Gregory?

'The tree lights' explained Tyler, lights that we put in a Christmas tree.' Gregory looked confused, which Tyler mistook for concerned. 'Well we did get a few lights' said Tyler.

'But why' asked Gregory? Now Tyler looked confused, 'we can't have a tree with no lights.'

'Well that would certainly be unique said Jenna, but lights make the tree look pretty'.

'Yes they do' declared Gregory. Now everyone looked confused. But why would you go to the mainland to look for lights, for a tree, that's here when trees have their own lights.' Everyone stilled looked confused.

'Like the trees in the mountain' asked Tyler?

'But this isn't the same kind of plant, said Ben I don't think it will work.'

'I don't think it matters, said Gregory, all trees have their own lights.' 'They do,' Jenna asked? 'Yes of course said Gregory or else how could we see where we're going, we often wondered why the village trees were not lit at night.'

'Do you mean that all trees can light up' asked Jenna?

'That's what I've been trying to tell you' said Gregory, a little exasperated.

Jake quickly jumped to his feet and ran out of the kitchen before anyone could ask why. He quickly returned carrying a potted tree from the front window of the bakery. 'Could you make this light up Gregory?'

'I don't see why not' came the reply.'

'How is it done' asked Jenna anxiously.'

'You just have to find the right roots, and give them a tweak,' said Gregory, as he hopped into the large pot and scurried down inside, some dirt flew out on to the floor, Millie frowned, but in a few moments the tree suddenly lit up and Gregory popped back up. The base of each leaf stem seemed to light up.

'Oh my soul' exclaimed Millie.

'That's amazing' said Jenna.

'Cool' said Matt.

'Yea, said Tyler, that's just what it looked like in the mountain, everywhere.'

'And you thought the mainland city was cool' asked Matt??

'So you think you can do this with the tree in the square' asked Jenna?

'If it has roots said Gregory I don't see why not.' 'But the roots of that tree will be bigger said Jake, a lot bigger and maybe not so easy to connect.'

'That shouldn't be a problem said Gregory, there will be smaller ones leading off the bigger ones, do you want me to go do it now' he asked eager to please. 'No said Jake we'll try it tomorrow in the day time so it won't show so much but we'll still know if it worked.'

'But early, added Ben, before the town is up.' Jake nodded in agreement.

'In the meantime said Millie we'll have to think up some kind of story for where we got the lights and why they are on all the time.'

'They don't have to be on all the time said Gregory, watch,' as he scurried into the soil again and turned off the lights. 'Perfect' claimed Jenna. 'You're simply amazing' said Millie as she brushed Gregory off and gave him a piece of cheese. I think you might have just saved this town.'

'You're pretty amazing too Millie, said Ben, you said one step at a time and sure enough the next step came.' Millie was all flustered but managed a 'thank you and how about some dessert, I think this calls for a celebration' she said as she got up from the table to get some pie, trying to hide her blushing cheeks.

The next day Gregory was able to get the tree to light up just like he said it would and Jake and Ben and the others were really starting to get excited about it. That evening they sat around the kitchen table drawing sketches and writing down ideas, grateful that no one else signed up for the decorating committee so they wouldn't have to explain about the lights.

'What wonderful ideas said Millie, oh this is going to look spectacular.'

'But we'll keep it all a secret' said Jenna, agreed? Everyone heartily agreed. 'So, said Tyler were gonna have lights in the tree and the houses and the mice will go in the tree but how are we going to keep the cats out of the tree?' Everyone looked worried but Gregory. 'That's easy he said touch one of those lights on tree. 'Oh said Tyler pulling his finger back quickly, I got a little shock.' 'It will be even worse for cats because their much smaller, Duchess touched one once it bothered her for days.' 'That's right' added Ben. 'But won't you get shocked too' asked Matt? 'No we've lived with them all our lives and never been hurt by them, smiled Gregory feeling special.

'I think they have a coating on their fur that protects them said Ben as did the weasels.'

'Well, I think we might actually have a chance of winning this year said Millie.'

'The town could sure use it said Jenna, but what if someone tries to touch the tree and complains of the shock, they might think it's unsafe and we might have some explaining to do.'

Everyone thought for a moment. I'll just say I wired it that way to prevent birds, cats and other animals from getting into the tree and messing it up, replied Jake.

'We'll put a little fence around with a warning sign' added Ben.

'Brilliant,' declared Millie!

'I have another idea for the tree but first I'll have to go back to the mainland said Ben it will be a surprise if it works.'

'Can we come' asked Tyler excited?

'Not this time answered Ben, I think I'll go Monday and you'll be in school.'

'Preparing for those exams added Jenna. Tyler gave her a scowl.

'But I could use your help Jake' added Ben.

'Sure' said Jake

# Chapter Ten

## The Proposal

Monday around 6:30 p.m. Ben and Jake returned from the main land with a large box, a few other parcels, and a surprise for Tyler that he planned to hide at Jakes place for Christmas. He also had a special little box in his pocket for Millie. As they rounded the corner they noticed a truck parked in front of the bakery.

'Wonder who that is,' asked Jake? Ben didn't answer but he had a bad feeling about this and was anxious to get in. As they entered they saw Frank grasping Millie's wrist, 'I'm not letting go until you say you'll go to the Christmas ball with me!' Millie was furious. 'I don't appreciate being held against my will, nor being told what to do now let go' she said as she broke free 'and get out.' Jenna and Tyler came running out from the kitchen and that's when Frank also noticed that Ben and Jake had just entered, all having just heard Millie's reply.

'What's going on asked Ben, a little angry as he and Jake moved over to Millie. Frank backed up a little but he wasn't ready to give up just yet, 'you really ask too much of her Ben.'

'I haven't asked anything of her' Ben replied.

'Exactly said Frank you probably haven't even asked her to the ball. You know all the time you were gone she waited for you, and now that you are back you're staying over at Jakes. What's the matter Ben are you not up to being a husband again?' Everyone wanted to kick him out but Ben got to him first with his fist. Then he grabbed him by the collar, pulled him up off the floor and nailed him to the wall, with his feet dangling 'hold him here,' he said to Jake. Jake easily held him to the spot.

'Are you going to hit me again' Frank asked with a bloody nose?

'No! Said Ben, there's something I want you to see. Ben walked over to Millie, 'I never wanted you to be alone Millie, but I also didn't want you to feel that just because I was back things had to be the same as they were before I left.' Millie was fighting hard to hold back the tears. Then Ben got down on one knee, I thought if I had a chance, perhaps I should start over again; he pulled out a little blue velvet box and opened it to show a very pretty diamond ring. Will you marry me, again?' Ben couldn't breathe until she answered. Millie couldn't hold back the tears any longer.

'Ben, I don't want to get married again.' Ben's eyes dropped along with his heart.

Millie continued, 'we had a perfect wedding and I always honoured it, I just want you back.'

Now Ben had tears in his eyes as Millie fell into his arms. Time froze for a moment, then everybody took a deep breath. Millie and Ben smiled through their tears as they stood up. Ben had forgotten that Jake was still holding Frank. 'You can let him go now.'

'Uh oh right' said Jake who had also forgotten he was holding him. Everyone looked at Frank and he could feel the shame and weight of it all. 'I'm sorry, he said I won't bother you again,' he lowered his head and walked out the door. Millie smiled at Ben who wasn't sure what to do with the ring in his hand. 'It's a beautiful ring' said Millie.

'Do you want it' asked Ben, not sure what to do with it?

'Of course said Millie, how many women do you know get proposed to by their husbands? It makes me feel, special.'

'You are special Millie, worth more than all the gold and diamonds in the world.' Millie hugged him. 'You're going to make me cry again, she said. As she stepped back she added, this will be a symbol of our new life together. She held out her hand and Ben slid the ring on her ring finger, it fit perfectly of course and went nice along with her wedding band. 'I love it' she said.

'You have to celebrate Jenna said, right this way your table waits. She walked to the cozy table in the corner. Please have a seat and your dinner will be right out. Ben and Millie smiled as they took a seat and everyone else went to the kitchen. O.K. said Jenna, first, Tyler, get some silverware, the nice ones, Jake, take that tree out front and set it by their table, and Gregory, could you work your magic please. Sure said Gregory honoured that he was asked to help.

'Then Tyler I want you to turn off all other lights.'

'O.k. but why' asked Tyler?

'Never mind' said Jenna,

'But they won't be able to see their food.'

'Just do it!'

Ben and Millie were holding hands across the table as Jake came out with a tree. Jake made on like he didn't see them holding hands, which was easy to do cause the tree was in front of him. Gregory lit it up and it made for a very romantic atmosphere.

'Sorry to leave you in the dark, said Tyler as he turned out the lights, but it's Jenna's orders he said sarcastically as Gregory hopped into Tylers pocket. Ben winked at Gregory and Gregory proudly smiled back. Tyler dumped their fanciest silver and napkins on the table.

'Millie can you sort this out I don't know how they're suppose to go and if it's not right Jenna will kill me.'

'Of course' she laughed.

Matt and Jenna brought out a cart with the roast beef special and Bens favourite Blueberry pie for dessert.

Just leave everything here when you're done, we'll clean it up in the morning said Jenna as she shooed everyone else back to the kitchen. Now what asked Tyler? Now you two study for the exam tomorrow and I'll get Jake some supper.

'Actually, said Jake we ate before we got on the ferry, thanks but I got a truck load of stuff to deliver to my place.'

'Well take this too said Jenna, handing him a box of food, a meat pie and some sweets. Millie was going to send it over anyways.'

'Thank you' said Jake.

'We can help', said Tyler.

'No said Jenna, Matt told his mother that you two were studying together tonight so I want you to get to it, and if you have any questions just ask.'

'I have a question' said Tyler with his hand raised as though he were in school.

'No I cannot give you the questions that are on the test' answered Jenna before he asked.

Tyler scowled as he lowered his hand. Jake chuckled as he walked out the door, grateful that Jenna had kept Tyler busy because he didn't know how he was going to keep that big box hidden till Christmas.

'This was delicious said Ben as they finished their supper, Millie smiled, there's something else I want to ask you.'

'What's that asked Millie.'

'Will you go to the ball with me?'

Millie smiled, 'I'll have to think about it she said, I did have another offer you know.'

Ben wasn't expecting that and he looked totally confused but then caught on and smiled.

'O.k. I'll go on one condition she continued.'

'Anything' said Ben playing along.

Millie took a deep breath, 'I'll go on the condition that you stay … here … tonight and from now on.'

Ben really wasn't expecting that. He didn't know what to say. 'Ah, are you sure' he asked?

'If you'd rather not, said Millie I hear Priscilla Andrews has her eye on you.'

It was true that Priscilla Andrews often left her dress shop to trot across the street to the Tool Barn just to see Ben, but he never caught on, he just thought her husband sent her and never even knew her name, but Millie and Jenna caught on. They knew Priscilla had a reputation for stealing husbands and would think that Ben was an easy target, but when they asked Ben about her visit, at first he didn't remember and when he did he said he found her a bit annoying but tried to be nice which was true.

'Millie, I just didn't want to pressure you, and I don't give a damn what Priscilla, a, a what's her name thinks. Millie was stunned but also pleased that Ben didn't care enough to remember Priscilla's last name. I . . . I love you Millie, he said in a much softer tone, I can't believe I actually have a second chance . . . with you.'

'Oh Ben I love you too' said Millie as she hugged him.

Ben did go to Jake's place later but it was only to get his things, which Jake had packed and waiting for him.

'Just had a feeling he said when Ben came over. I'm happy for you but I'm sorry to see you go.' 'It was the only way she'd go to the Ball with me' said Ben. Jake laughed. 'Hey Jake, have you ever thought of asking Jenna to the Ball?' Jake was silent for a moment, as he was about to reveal his deepest secret.

'I have thought of it, often, but I never felt . . . like I had a right to.'

'But why' asked Ben.

'I guess I . . . well there are a lot of guys out there who . . . I'm just not good at this kind of thing, and she probably would rather . . . there's lots of guys better than me.'

'That's not true Jake, I didn't raise you to believe in such nonsense and if it were true, where are they, all those other guys; she doesn't go out with anyone, does she? Think about it Jake, I gotta get back before Millie thinks I've changed my mind.'

Jake smiled as Ben hurried out the door. He wasn't sure what to think about what Ben said but he would think about it, he would think about it all night. Jenna seemed more like a sister to him, but she also seemed distant as though she didn't want to be around him. Jake was never sure how to read her. But Ben was right, there were no other guys around her, maybe she just didn't have time for guys in her life right now, she was quite busy these days, school, the bakery, and the Christmas preparations. But surely she'd want to go to the ball with someone.

Before Jake finally drifted off to sleep at 4:00 A.M. he decided that he would ask Jenna to the dance, it might take him a few days to work up the courage but what did he have to lose, he didn't think things could get much worse, she barely spoke to him now, only when she had to, was she still angry over the snob sisters, that didn't seem like her. What if she was upset that he hadn't asked her out? Either way he had to know and he would ask her when the time was right, he still had a few weeks before the Ball.

Now that he had made that decision he actually felt lighter, and confident, as though this was something he should have done long ago and was finally getting to it. He felt relieved as though he could actually get a few hours sleep and it seemed to be all he needed.

After a couple of hours, Jake woke up energised as though he had slept the whole night, eager to look for just the right opportunity to approach Jenna. But that opportunity never came that day as she was quite busy and when she wasn't, there were always other people around. Now that he got up enough courage to ask her out there was no way he could do it in front of anyone else and well there was still three weeks.

# Chapter Eleven

## The Date

The snob sisters showed up now and then at the tool barn looking for Jake, when someone mentioned he was working on the tree they would show up there, but being high up on the ladder, he could see them coming and Jake would go for a walk till they left.

'You'll have to stand up to them some day' said Ben.

'Yea said Jake right now I don't have the time,' luckily for him they gave up coming, they had their own Christmas preparations to make, shop, shop, shop.

The next week flew by because in the large box that they had brought back from the main land was the largest set of train tracks anyone had ever seen, well actually it was more than one set it was five. Ben also bought some nice trains to go with it. It was his idea to put it in the tree, not under the tree, but in the tree starting at the top and spiralling down and around till it got to the bottom. It took a lot of work but Jake loved the idea, it certainly was original and what kept them even busier, and made it even more original was Millie's idea to make replicas of houses not only of Pleasantville but also of Midville and Richville. Including them as part of their Christmas was a way of creating unity which was the Govenors Christmas theme.

Jenna got busy making some Christmas outfits for the mice. Between her school work, the bakery, painting houses and sewing, she seemed to fly from place to place and could be a little irritated at times if anyone got in her way. School was the worst of it though with kids barely paying attention and hyper active with anticipation for the comming Holliday. It was like this every year and usually Jenna had no problem dealing with it, but this year, with everything else on her plate she was barely holding it together. She snapped at people when they suggested she take a break, even Ben got snapped at. It made Jake wish he didn't put off asking her the big question, it didn't look like he was ever going to get a chance now.

Tyler stopped speaking to her altogether and avoided her. He didn't even act up in her class like he usually did, today three children were sent to the principal's office for trivial stuff she usually handled herself.

Even the staff noticed that she was stressed and brought up her behavior in the staff meeting after school. 'WELL she said as she stood up, if more people in this town would work together it would certainly make things easier for others!'

She knew the real reason they didn't want to work on the Christmas tree project was because each year those who did got their picture put in the news papers, on the island and on the main land. In years past it was a real embarrassment to have your picture put in as a loser at Christmas.

'Well what can we do' asked one genuinely concerned teacher.

'Never mind said Jenna, we've got it taken care of she snapped as she stormed out.

She didn't really want anyones help nor to give away any of their secrets she just wanted to get home and they were in her way so they got 'Jen blasted,' as Tyler was calling it these days, behind her back of course.

The one thing that bothered her more than all the work she had to do was that Jake didn't ask her to the Ball, nor did anyone else, it was just a week away now, and she knew it was all her fault for the way she had been acting. But still she felt that if he didn't ask her out this year, he never would.

Ben and Jake had seen her rushing by wiping her eyes. 'That's it said Ben this has gotten out of hand.' He and Jake got down off their ladders and headded for the bakery. Millie met them at the door. 'I know I know she said listening to their concerns, that's why tonight were taking a break to have a special dinner. The houses are finished, her sewing is nearly done and I've done all the baking I'm doing for Christmas. I've prepared her favourite it will be a reward for all her hard work, a little celebration for us all.'

Ben took Millies face in his hands, 'you're an angel Millie a real God send,' and he gave her a kiss on the lips. She was a little embarrassed as there were still customers in the shop.

Jake went home to put away some tools and clean up for supper. He came to the conclusion that if anyone were going to ask her out they would have done so by now and that tonight's dinner would be a good time to ask her, even if he had to do it in front of her family it wouldn't be so bad, they were his family too and they might even encourage her to go out with him if she were indecisive. Jake began to get his hopes up again and was feeling pretty good as he walked across the street to the bakery. But once again his hopes deflated as Jenna refused to come out of her room. She had a stack of exams to mark and that was her excuse. She didn't want to see anyone. Finally Millie gave up and brought up a plate of food for her which she barely touched.

Ben decided he would go and talk to her but just as he rose from his seat; a knock came at the door. Ben was surprised to see Mayor Edwards from Richville and his son Byron, standing at the door. 'Richard, he said is that you.'

'Ben, it's been a long time, you look well.' Mayor Edwards had taken a liking to Ben and Jake ever since they had done some renovations in his house and at the town hall. He wouldn't call anyone else for the job, they were the best on the island and better than those on the mainland as well. They really cared about their work and the people they worked for.

'Come in, come in said Ben how good to see you again, care for a bite to eat?'

'Well' said Mayor Edwards I wouldn't mind a piece of Millie's pie, you'd think someone in Richville would know how to make pie, I have fond memories of when you and Jake used to bring me a pie and I would hide it and save it for myself.'

'Oh my soul said Millie well you sit right there and I'll get you some.' She was back in a flash with three baked pies and a slice for the Mayor and his son.

And is this your son asked Ben?

Yes, Byron, you remember him?

All grown up now said Ben where does the time go.

I know said the Mayor, Byron is now head of the psychiatry department at the hospital.

'And Jake how are you doing these days, the Mayor asked?'

'Good, thank you,' was all Jake said. Jake had a bad feeling in the pit of his stomach and was a little anxious to know what they were up to.

'So what brings you here Richard, was it just Millie's pies? Jake and I are a little over booked right now.'

'Yes I'm sure you are said the Mayor sincerely but actually it was Miss Hopkins I came to see.' 'Jenna, asked Tyler?' 'You don't want to see her.'

'Tyler! scolded Millie. She's just been a little stressed out with everything on her plate Millie explained.'

'Is she here? Asked the Mayor?'

'Yes of course I'll go get her.'

Jenna told Millie she didn't care if it was the Govenor or the King who wanted to see her; she was deep into her work and wasn't leaving so they'd have to come to her. Poor Millie was a little shocked and didn't quite know how to put it to the mayor. She's extremely busy marking exams but said she would see you if you could come up.'

'O.k. said the Mayor I understand. Common' he said to his son who had been quiet but followed hesitantly.

Millie led them up the stairs to Jenna's room, knocked on the door then entered to find Jenna still sitting at her desk. Jenna looked up shocked to see not only the Mayor of Richville but also his son, which she met briefly once, standing there in her room. She thought Millie was just playing a trick on her to get her to come down. She stood up quickly and straightened her hair and clothes.

'Oh, ah . . . um . . .' she didn't know how to start.

The Mayor saved her, 'pardon the intrusion he said, but this was rather important.'

'Of course' said Jenna, quickly moving her things off the couch by the wall, 'please sit down.' The Mayor and his son sat on the couch, Jenna pulled out her desk chair and Millie sat herself in the arm chair not that she was invited to, but nothing could pull her away right now.

Actually Jenna was kind of glad she was there.

'What can I do for you' Jenna asked?

'Well said the Mayor it's something you can do for Richville.'

Jenna smiled sarcastically, 'I can't imagine what I could possibly do for Richville, unless, if you need a teacher, and I'm not available. I wouldn't leave Pleasantville no matter how much you offered me.'

'It isn't that said the Mayor, anxious to get this over with, I wanted to ask, and I hope I'm not too late but do you have a date to the ball?'

Jenna and Millie both were surprised and confused.

'Ah, aren't you married' replied Jenna?

'Oh sakes alive, said the Mayor it's not for me it's for my son Byron.' Jenna looked at Byron questioningly. He was looking at the floor.

'Right said Jenna let me see if I got this straight. You had to come all the way to Pleasantville to find a date for your son?' The Mayor nodded.

'First of all, continued Jenna, I hardly believe that he needs his dad to find him a date and I won't be paraded around in front of Richville for all your people to laugh at.'

'And lastly, she said looking at Byron, he doesn't seem too excited about the idea either.'

'Let me explain said the Mayor. First of all I like your attitude there's not enough people who speak their mind.'

'I know' said Jenna thinking about Jake. Millie also knew who she was thinking about.

'Second, he continued, I am not in the habit of finding dates for my son, he has a girlfriend.' 'What??!!!?' asked Jenna totally confused and a little upset. Byron finally spoke up.

'He's right, I have a girlfriend and she's not going to like this, why can't you find a date for the girls they seem to have taken a fancy to Jake. They're at his place right now.' They could see from Jenna's bedroom window Gertrude and Matilda knocking on Jakes door.

'I like Jake too said the Mayor; he's done a lot of good work for me, I don't want to punish him for it, (Jenna smirked,) and that's exactly why I am not going to put him through that misery, as much as I love my daughters I'm afraid it would be poor business for me to pone them off on one of the other towns. It would make it seem like we don't care very much about them and we do, really.'

'I'm afraid, said Jenna that you haven't convinced me of that.'

'Let me explain, please, the Mayor implored. You know that the Govenor's Christmas theme this year is unity.' Jenna and Millie both nodded.

'At our council meeting it was decided that the best idea we had to promote unity was if someone from my family and each of my councilmens families escorted someone from Midville and Pleasantville to the dance.'

'But Cynthia is in Midville said Byron, why can't I just take her.'

'Your girlfriend is in Midville asked the Mayor?'

'Yes' Byron sighed.

'Oh dear does your mother know?'

'No' said Byron, I know she'd have a fit if I dated anyone outside of Richville.'

'Would that be Cynthia Norris' asked Jenna? Byron nodded.

'I know Cynthia said Jenna, we went to college together; she became a nurse. I think Byron's mother should be greatful that her son found such a wonderful careing individual.'

Byron couldn't help but smile. 'I couldn't agree more' said the Mayor trying to stay on Jenna's good side. 'But it's too late, the council decided that I should choose Pleasantville, for the sake of unity, they also decided that your sisters shall not have any part of this, for the sake of good public relations and, unity, Harrison got Midville.'

'I think you should worry more about the unity in your own family said Jenna.'

'I agree' said Byron.

'So do I,' sighed the Mayor 'but the fact remains that we still need someone from Pleasantville.' 'Won't your wife object to that' asked Jenna?

'Yes said the Mayor but it wasn't my choice. Jenna looked at him with raised eyebrows.

That's not what I meant he continued, I have some very good friends here regardless of what my wife thinks, oh I can see that this is useless I'll not trouble you anymore he said feeling defeated, I'm done here,' he said as he got up.

'Well I'm not said Jenna, sit down,' please. The Mayor sat back down, in a bit of a shock but grateful that Jenna never ran for Mayor of Richville, thinking that she could easily win even though she's from Pleasantville.

Byron was also impressed; no one ever told his father what to do not even his mother, he was finally starting to enjoy this visit.

First of all, said Jenna, what made you choose me?'

'The council chose you. Lillian Baxter and Judith Reece said you would be an excellent choice and from everything they told me about you I was quite impressed.'

'Judith and Lillian are good friends of ours said Millie.'

'That's how you were chosen' said the Mayor.

'Alright said Jenna, taking a deep breath, I'll do it. Byron looked to the floor. Don't look so discouraged Byron I have a plan and if it works it will benefit us both. And this is the only way I'll do this she said to the Mayor.'

'O.k. said the Mayor, whats your plan.'

'My plan is to,[she looked at Millie wondering what she would think], make Jake jealous, she turned to Byron, your sisters aren't the only ones who fancy him, Millie seemed anxious to hear more, 'and in the process, she continued, have your mother think that we have, fallen in love and are talking about marriage.' Byron looked confused, and a little worried.

Don't you see, said Jenna, if your mother thinks you're going to marry someone from Poorville, who's only after your money, she'll, she'll' . . .

'Explode' added Byron.

'Exactly said Jenna, then when she learns the truth she'll be only too happy to embrace Cynthia as one of the family. What do you think?'

'Brilliant!' Just brilliant' exclaimed Byron.

'I like it added the Mayor'

'But this must be kept secret, said Jenna it can't leave this room or else it may not work.'

'Did you ever think of running for office' asked the Mayor with a smile on his face?

'Maybe someday when I have nothing better to do,' replied Jenna.

Byron was shocked but the Mayor busted out laughing which surprised him even more.

Jenna and Millie laughed a little too.


'Jakes always impressed me as a very smart man, said the Mayor, I can't imagine why he hasn't already asked you to the ball.'

'Neither can I' complained Jenna.

'He's just a little shy' said Millie

'Well I really like this girl' said the Mayor.

'Yea said Byron can we trade her, two sisters for one?'

'Not on your life' laughed Millie.

'Let's start tomorrow' said the Mayor, smiling.

'How' asked Byron?

'Easy said the Mayor, you ask her over for dinner tomorrow night, to meet the family, this should be entertaining if nothing else.'

'I'll wear my shabbiest outfit' said Jenna excitedly.

'I'll pick you up at six' asked Byron?

'Six would be fine said Jenna, then she turned to Millie, so what do you think Millie, think you can keep this a secret from Jake?'

'I have been keeping your feelings secret from him for quite some time now said Millie a little puffed up, a little while longer shouldn't be a problem. And I must say it sure is nice to see you smile again.' Jenna smiled even more and gave Millie a hug.

'Well that settles it then, said the Mayor, we'll see you tomorrow night.'

'Tomorrow night' said Jenna.

'Oh I almost forgot said the Mayor, stopping at the door, this is for you, he handed her an envelope, all those who accept, receive a little reward.'

Jenna looked in the envelope; it was a stack of money, 'What am I suppose to do with this, buy a fancy gown or something?'

'I wouldn't dare tell you what to do with your money. I expect you might find a better use.

Jenna smiled as she sat the envelope on her desk, with no idea what to do with it. She and Millie walked Byron and his father down the stairs and to the front door.

'Ben, good seeing you again, said the Mayor, you must come over and visit sometime, you too Jake.'

'Sounds good' said Ben, Jake smiled and nodded. He thought now that they're leaving and Jenna is here and actually smiling, he'll finally get his chance to ask her out.

'See you tomorrow' said Byron to Jenna.

'Tomorrow said Jenna happily' as he and the Mayor walked out.

'What's happening tomorrow' asked Tyler?

'I have a date' answered Jenna.

All at once Tyler Matt and Ben said 'you have a date???' Jake would have said it too but he couldn't find his voice, he just sat there looking as though all the wind had been knocked out of him.

Jenna scowled at them. 'Yes I have a date and just why is that so hard to believe?!!!' She turned and walked off to the kitchen, to get a bite to eat, she hadn't touched the dinner Millie brought upstairs and didn't realise how hungry she was until now. Jake thanked Millie for the nice meal and went home. Ben offered to go with him to work a little more on some extra decorations but Jake said the day had wore him out and he was due for a good rest so Ben helped Millie clean up and the boys tended to the mice. Ben felt bad for Jake but decided it was best to stay out of it.

The next morning Jake was at the tree as soon as the sun came up, he hadn't slept well and wanted to keep his mind busy.
He didn't even go to the bakery for breakfast so Ben brought him some muffins and juice when he showed up about eight thirty. Jake didn't realise how hungry he had been till he bit into one of Millie's blueberry muffins.
'That's marvellous Ben said, you've got the train track just about done.' Ben decided he would find anything to talk about but Jenna, and Jake was grateful for his company.

At school Jenna was much happier, the staff was quite surprised. Even though the kids were getting louder each day with the approaching of Christmas, Jenna didn't mind, she even joined in the fun. Since exams were done and her report cards were ready and waiting to go home, she decided to throw a little party for her kids. She arrived early to decorate the classroom with streamers and even set up a little Christmas tree in the corner. She brought lots of sweets and party hats and had set up a table where kids could decorate their own cookies to take home. They could make decorations to hang on the tree, and Christmas cards for mom and dad.

Jenna had closed the classroom door and waited outside for all of the children to arrive. She apologised for the way she had been acting and wanted to make up for it. The kids were thoroughly shocked when she opened the door, but they thoroughly enjoyed the party.

Jenna even had Christmas music playing. She was having a great time herself. The two other teachers in her hall were a little envious, their classes had to listen to stories and draw pictures and they were totally bored so Jenna invited them to join in. She thought they might have company so she brought lots of extra sweets.

After lunch the teachers decided to separate classes again so they could each put on a little Christmas play for each other. The kids thought it was a great idea. One of the plays was about Santa's workshop and a clumsy little elf that Santa finally took under his wing and told him that when he was his age he was clumsy too. One class chose a skit about Rudolf the red nosed reindeer and Jenna chose the nativity scene skit. She had a lot to be grateful for and wanted the children to remember the real reason for Christmas. Even the principle came in for a visit and when he heard of the skits he asked the classes if they would mind putting their skits on in front of the whole school in the gym. The kids were excited to do it. Everyone had such a great day. Jenna felt like she was walking on air on her way home, She still had a bit of a bad feeling for the way she had acted gaining her the name of 'grumpy.' She decided that tonight when she was out with Byron, she would use the money that Mayor Edwards had given her to get a small gift for each of them to take home on their last day of school.

At ten to six Jenna came bouncing down the stairs dressed in her best dress.hoping Jake would see but he wasn't there. He was however looking out of his front shop window.

Jenna looked happier than she had in a long time he had to admit, even though he was so miserable. He knew Byron and always thought highly of him and felt deep inside, that this was probably good for Jenna.

'You look really good said Byron as he opened the door for her, a lot less scary than you did last night.' 'Thank you laughed Jenna, as she hopped into his car, but Jake isn't here to see us' she added after Byron got in his car.

'Oh he's watching said Byron; I can see him looking out his window in my review mirror.' 'Perfect' said Jenna.

'I thought you were supposed to wear shabby clothes,' asked Byron, 'that looks really nice.'

'And that's how I want Jake to see me, as though I'm trying to impress you. But I'm going to change at Cynthia's on our way to your place. She called me today and she likes our plan. She's going to do all she can to help us.'

'Yes I know said Byron, she was pretty excited when I told her about it last night, and she appreciated the kind things you said about her and she thinks you're brilliant.' Jenna smiled as they drove off.


'Come in' said Cynthia, anxious to see them. 'Where is everyone' asked Byron?

'Out Christmas shopping said Cynthia, have a seat.' Jenna sat in an arm chair and Byron sat with Cynthia and gave her a kiss on the cheek which she liked though it made her blush a little.

'So what did you think when Byron asked you out Jenna, she asked?

Jenna laughed a little, 'actually he had to get his dad to do it because he refused to.'

Cynthia laughed 'oh how sweet' as she took Byron's hand in hers.

'Yes he sat there like a pouting little boy who had just gotten detention continued Jenna, I know, I've seen that look many times.'

Cynthia laughed even harder, Jenna joined in even Byron had to admit it was pretty funny now that he looked back at it.

Soon Jenna was changed into her drabby plain green dress. 'Ooo' said Cynthia wrinkling her nose.

'I know said Jenna, I stopped off at the second hand store on my way home from school and bought a few lovely outfits just like this,' she giggled.

'Wonderful' said Cynthia, but your hair is too nice.' After tying Jenna's hair back in a pony tail she looked perfect.

'So, do you have a plan for when you get to Byron's asked Cynthia?' Byron looked confused. 'I've been going over a few things in my head said Jenna, how does this sound?

'Hi Mrs Edwards said Jenna grabbing Cynthia's hand and shaking it hard, Byron you didn't tell me you lived in a big ole castle. You all must have some big ole pile of money.'

'Oh that's perfect, cried Cynthia! Byron thought it was good too and was beginning to get the spirit of it. 'There's a big picture of my great aunt Lydia hanging in the foyer, she was my mother's favourite aunt but no one else liked her and she looks like a witch, she kind of resembles Gertrude. We call her the witch of Richville mother hates that, so be sure to insult the picture when you see it, you can't miss it.'

'O.k. laughed Jenna.

'And Byron, you have to act like Jenna is just the cutest thing you ever did see, said Cynthia. Put your arm around her every chance you get. Byron nodded. You'd better go I can't wait for you to get back here and tell me all about it.'

'Well here goes' said Jenna as they walked up the steps to the Mayors house.

'Don't worry, said Byron, Dads given everyone strict orders to treat you well and be on their best behaviour, it wouldn't look good to have you poorly treated in Richville.' Jenna smiled as Byron's words gave her courage.

'Everyone this is Jenna Hopkins.' Byron's sisters looked her over and smirked, that's all they would dare do with their father there. Mrs Edwards looked from poor Jenna to Byron who put on his biggest smile then to her husband.

'Lovely' she said in a sarcastic voice.

'May I take your coat miss' the butler asked?

'I doubt it will fit you Jenna smiled but if you promise to give it back Ill let you borrow it for a while.'

The poor man raised his eye brows as he didn't know how to respond to that.

Byron helped Jenna off with her coat and handed it over to the butler, along with his own. The butler looked to the Mayor who nodded and then he walked off. Byron and his dad looked at eachother surpressing a laugh.

The dining room doors opened. Dinners ready announced another servant Byron led Jenna over to the table; she had never seen anything quite so fancy. The first course was soup. Jenna made it obvious that she was copying everyone else in choosing from one of the many utensils that lay before her, looking them over carefully then looking to Byron to see which one he would choose, and picking the same one. Of course she knew which one to use but the snob sisters didn't know that.

Gertrude gave her a smirk with a grunt and Henrietta giggled, of course they both straightened right up as their father cleared his throat.

'Well that was great I'm plum full, Jenna said, knowing full well that was only the first course, then she saw the servants come in with the main course; oh' she said and smiled a little, trying to look embarrassed.

No one was talking they seemed to want to get this over with as soon as possible, each for their own reasons. Gertrude and Henrietta already hated Jenna and were quite put out that they couldn't say anything nasty to her. Mrs Edwards was visibly upset and the Mayor was nervous about their little scheme but he had to admit that Jenna seemed to be pulling it off quite well. She ate as fast as she could making it seem as though she hadn't eaten in a while then dessert came out. 'Oh my soul she said don't you people ever stop eating?' Everyone looked at her in surprise. Both Gertrude and Henrietta stared with their mouths hung open dying to say something, but again, a stern look from their father made them mind their own business. Mrs Edwards looked at her son with raised eyebrows but Byron happily smiled back and said, 'she's cute isn't she?'

Mrs Edwards then looked as though she were in shock and the Mayor tried not to choke on his dessert. Jenna kept right on eating and thoroughly enjoying her dessert, looking as though she were oblivious to all the silent fuss that was being made around her, when actually she knew she had them, hook, line and sinker.

'Oh that was so good I think I died and went to heaven, what do you call that? I have to tell my Aunt Millie about it.'

'I believe its called Bavarian Cream Pie said the Mayor, and to show our appreciation for your company this evening I will have Percy box one up for you to take home for Aunt Millie.' 'Really?' said Jenna as her eyes almost popped out of her head.

'Really,' smiled the Mayor trying not to laugh.

'Well thank you all for a wonderful evening said Jenna, but I really must be going now.' There was silence as no one protested.

'But you'll come back and see us soon asked the Mayor?'

'Oh I'll come back often said Jenna as Percy handed her a boxed pie, you have all been so wonderful to me, thank you she said as they walked out to the foyer. I can't wait to see the look on Millie's face when I' . . . just then she let out a loud scream and dropped the pie, which opened and splattered all over Henrietta's dress and the floor. Henrietta gasped and was about to cry out but one look from her father silenced her.

'What is it asked Byron, are you ok?'

'A, a, a witch?!!?? Said Jenna pointing a shakey finger to the picture of his great ugly aunt, the one he had mentioned earlier. Byron had forgotten about it and she didn't notice it when they arrived but when they left the dineing room there it was stareing her right in the face, making you feel like an unwelcomed guest. 'It gave me such a start.' Henrietta was about to laugh but one look from her mother silenced her again.

'THAT!!! said Mrs Edwards, losing all patience, is my great aunt Lydia Beatrice Jenkins. I was given her name and was her favourite till the day she died!

'Oh, I'm so sorry' said Jenna trying to look sincere. It almost looked as though Mrs Edwards was about to cry.

'I really am sorry and just look at the mess I've gone and made.'

'Not to worry we'll get this cleaned up, and Percy will get you another pie said the Mayor as he walked Jenna and Byron to the door, and out to the car.

'That was brilliant' exclaimed Byron.

'I really am sorry about that' said Jenna.

'Oh please, replied the Mayor, I can't thank you enough, you did me a huge favour.'

'I did' asked Jenna?

'Yes you most certainly did.'

'And here's your reward Miss' said Percy as he handed her another pie.

'Thank you' said Jenna looking confused.

'You see said Mayor Edwards, Lydia and I had an agreement that if one more person was frightened by her Aunts picture then that picture would have to be moved. It has caused some embarrassing moments.'

'I'm sure it has said Jenna, it really was quite scary.'

'And we can finally be rid of it added Mayor Edwards.

'Halleluiah said Percy, the Mayor smiled at him; well the foyer will look a lot better without it.'

'You're right, said the Mayor and I've got just the picture to replace it.

I hope my family didn't scare you off' said the Mayor as they reached the car.

'No said Jenna I have a little shopping to do before I get back and I was going to ask Byron if he wouldn't mind taking me.'

'Sure said Byron where would you like to go?

'To a toy store I want to get a toy for each child in my class. For some it will be the only toy they get this year.'

'Yes I know said the Mayor, that storm hit your village hard. Hey, why don't you leave that to me, how many children in your school?'

'My school' asked Jenna???

There are two hundred and twenty seven exactly' said Jenna but . . .'

'No no said the Mayor, I insist, they'll be delivered first thing in the morning.

'The whole school????'

'I'll call principle Martin to find out how many boys how many girls . . .'

'This wouldn't have anything to do with the Christmas contest and spreading unity and all that, would it,' Jenna asked?

'Actually that is a good idea said the Mayor, I must do the same for the Midville schools, you are brilliant, but the real reason I wanted to do this for you is because you did such a big favour for me.'

Cynthia roared with laughter as Byron and Jenna recounted the evening to her especially the part about dear Aunt Lydia.

'I have to admit said Byron, we were terrified of her as kids, and we never even met her, even now if I have to walk past her portrait at night, in the dim light, I do it quickly.'

'Oh my poor baby,' said Cynthia as she hugged him. 'This is going to work I know it, she said. Now Byron it's your turn to put on a show.'

'O.k. what do I do.'

'When you take Jenna home, Cynthia continued as she took Byrons hand and stood up, I want you to hug her like this and linger for just a moment then I want you to give her a kiss on the cheek, watch as she goes in and then leave.'

'Are you sure' asked Byron?

'Completely said Cynthia it's the only way this will work and you'd better be as convincing as Jenna was, and tomorrow you'll send a lovely bouquet of flowers saying how much you enjoyed the evening, and ask her out for another date. Does that sound allright with you Jenna?'

'It sounds like you could write a romance novel, she replied, I just hope all your scheaming isn't for nothing. What if Jake isn't watching.'

'He will be said Cynthia I know this is going to work I can feel it said Cynthia. Now you'd better get going before my family get home and wonder why my boyfriend is dating you.'

Jenna and Byron followed Cynthia's directions to a tee. I think Cynthia was right said Byron as he stepped back from hugging Jenna, Jake just turned out the upstairs light. Jenna smiled, I think you'd better send Cynthia a lovely bouquet of flowers tomorrow as well and write on the card how brilliant you think she is and how fortunate you are to have such a wonderful girl.'

Byron smiled, 'you girls do come up with some great ideas.'

# Chapter Twelve

## The Envelope

The next day Jenna received the flowers and the school received an amazing two hundred and twenty seven Christmas presents as promised. The excitement spread through the whole school, but Jenna noticed that there was one child missing, he had missed a lot of school. His mother said he wasn't feeling well so Jenna decided that she would take him his gift and invited Tyler and Matt to come along. They were only too happy to do it; it had been a while since they had seen Billy and they looked forward to seeing him again. They couldn't wait to give him his present but when they arrived they found Mrs Walters, Billy's mother in tears.

'The doctor called yesterday, Billy has a tumor, she sobbed, he needs an operation, it's dangerous, she cried harder, and eight hundred dollars? Where do I get that kind of money?'
'We'll get it somehow, said Jenna as she hugged Mrs Walters. Why don't you boys bring Billy his present said Jenna, it looks like Mrs Walters could use a good cup of tea.' Mrs Walters nodded and sniffed, 'upstairs first door on the right she said. He might be sleeping, he sleeps a lot but he'll be happy to see you, thank you so much for coming boys' she said as tears leaked down her face. Tyler and Matt nodded and went upstairs. Billy was just waking up. He was so excited to see the boys again that some of the color came back into his cheeks. Matt and Tyler thought it best not to say anything about what they had just heard so they had a good time playing with their Christmas presents, three big trucks. The walk home was quiet. The boys wondered if

they would ever see their friend again and Jenna wondered where the money would come from.

Millie was excited to see them all arrive; she had baked a special, last day of school cake and was anxious to show it off, but became concerned when she saw the long faces and no one felt like cake. The boys went to tend to the mice and Jenna explained to Millie.

'I know, said Millie, she asked for some stew hoping that would make him feel better and Ive been sending some over every day but not even my soup can help that, a tumor, oh the poor dear.'

'Well said Jenna I'm going to put this school stuff away and I'll be right back to help with supper.' Jenna went to her room and as she put her purse on her dresser she noticed the envelope that the Mayor had given her the other night. Quickly she grabbed it thinking this could help Mrs Walters some. Jenna hadn't counted it till now and was shocked to see that there was a thousand dollars. She thought maybe a hundred or two, but never dreamed there would be a thousand dollars in that envelope. She kicked off her heels threw on her sneakers grabbed the envelope and ran down to show Millie who was just as shocked. 'What are you going to do with it' she asked? 'It's going to the Walters family Jenna answered, Mayor Edwards said I could do whatever I wanted with it and I can't think of anything better.' 'Neither can I, said Millie, here take this too' she said as she bagged a couple of meat pies, rolls and sweets.

Jenna hurried over to the Walters home. Mr Walters answered the door. It was obvious that he was exaughsted and totally discouraged but he invited her in. 'Mary's upstairs with Billy he said giving him his medication.'

'Is someone here William,' said Mrs. Walters as she came down the stairs. 'Hi said Jen, Millie sent over some food, she thought you might be busy and could use a break and I wanted to talk to you about Billy.'

'I know he's missed a lot of school' said Mr. Walters ...

'It's not that said Jenna, we'll help him get caught up, it's the operation I wanted to talk about.' Mr Walters gave a sigh as he sat down on the worn couch, staring at the floor so none would notice his tear brimming eyes.

'Please have a seat' said Mrs Walters as she sat by her husband. Jenna sat in a chair.

'There's nothing you can do' said Mr Walters wiping his nose. 'Please forgive us said Mrs Walters wiping her eyes it's been so hard, he's our only child' she said crying harder. Mr. Walters put his arm around her. 'There's not even anything this town can do. Iv'e been to see the Mayor, there's just no money, we need a miracle.' The sight before Jenna's eyes almost broke her heart.

'I believe in miracles she said, here this is for you.' She took the envelope out of her pocket and handed it to Mr Walters. He couldn't believe his eyes; he passed it to his wife.

'A thousand dollars' said Jenna. 'What???'said Mrs Walters. 'But how???'

Jenna explained all about Mayor Edwards and his idea about the Christmas Ball and so on. 'I thought it was only a hundred or two. I never looked in the envelope before now, I actually forgot about it till I got home today.'

'Are you sure about this,' said Mr Walters?

'Absolutely,' said Jenna. 'Who needs a thousand dollars for a dress?'

'But the operation is only eight hundred' he replied.

'Yes said Jenna, you'll need some travel money, it isn't much, perhaps we could have a fund raiser. I'll think of something, she said.'

'I don't know how to thank you' said Mr Walters.

'I have thanks enough' said Jenna who was on cloud nine.

Mrs Walters gave her a big hug with tears in her eyes, happy tears this time.

As Jenna neared home she saw Byron's car parked out front. 'Byron,' she said as she entered and saw him sitting alone in the empty bakery. Millie came out front at the same time.
'Did you forget our date already asked Byron?'
'Oh that's my fault said Millie, I didn't have a chance to tell her you called, or show her the flowers.'
'Oh right said Jenna, Cynthia wanted us to get together tonight to go over more plans, I did forget, last day of school and all.' She decided not to tell him about the money just yet.
Byron smiled and nodded though his profession as a psychiatrist had taught him how to recognise when someone wasn't being totally truthful.
'Your father sent the toys and the children went wild,' Jenna continued, 'It was all wonderful though. So what time is Cynthia expecting us?'
'Not for an hour or two said Byron, she's doing some shopping, and Mom's still going on about last night's disaster, as she calls it and my sisters are right behind her calling you every name in the book I'm afraid, Jenna laughed, nothing could bring her down today, so I thought I'd come over early, in case Jake was hanging around.'
'He was here earlier said Millie, until that beautiful bouquet of flowers showed up.' Jenna looked to the counter, 'wow' she said.
'I read the card out loud of course and he left. Since you two have some time why don't you stay here and I'll bring out supper.'
'We can come out to the kitchen' said Jenna as she stood up.
'You could said Millie with a hand on Jenna's shoulder forcing her back down but with that curtain opened Jake

has good view of the two of you from his place and I'll bet he's watching you right now.'

'Millie, you're very sly, claimed Byron, you could work for my dad.'

'I've got better things to do' she laughed as she walked off to the kitchen.

'So, said Jenna, did Aunt Lydia come down off her wall?'

'She did, replied Byron with a laugh she was down by the time I got home and a nice scenery picture of Richville put up in its place. My dad had it painted and just waiting in his office ready to jump on that wall at a moment's notice.

I started coming down the stairs and I noticed Mom staring at the picture she kind of likes it; she's been stopping to look at it all day. Dad even caught her smiling at it, he apologised if it hurt her feelings. She said it did but she also feels that the picture of Richville was very well done and much more appropriate for a Mayors house. Dad gave her an early Christmas present, a necklace, said he bought it for her to wear to the Ball. She loved it and, well, I snuck out the back way. Do you believe in Miracles Jenna?'

Again Jenna thought about the Money and the Walters.

'Yes I do' she said.

'That witch has been on that wall since I was born and I thought it would be there till the day I died, said Byron, you're some kind of miracle worker. Jenna laughed. They had their supper, Byron thanked Millie and said it was better than home, Millie blushed and Byron and Jenna went off to Cynthia's.

Just wait till you see what I got today she said as she pulled them up to her room, which was twice the size of Jenna's. She sat them each in a chair facing big double doors. Cynthia pulled them open to reveal the most beautiful gown Jenna had ever laid eyes on.

'Oh my' said Jenna.

'Do you like it' asked Cynthia?

'Oh it's the most beautiful thing I have ever seen.'

'It's pretty nice' said Byron.

'Pretty nice???? complained Cynthia who was hoping for more than that.

'Oh what do guys know about a dress unless a girl is in it declared Jenna. Go on, put it on.'

'Cynthia closed the doors to her large closet which was also a dressing room, complete with chair make up table and large mirror a minute later she opened them again. 'Wow' said Byron. 'Now that's the reaction I was looking for' affirmed Cynthia. Byron was glad he pleased her but he was actually thinking, wow, something doesnt look right. It's true that the beautiful violet chiffon gown with the sparkles clashed against her beautiful pale skin and long luxorious red hair, everything was beautiful; it just didn't work together.'

But Byron wasn't about to burst her bubble, he wouldn't know how to put that into words if he tried. 'It's beautiful' said Jenna, who was feeling the same way Byron was, even Cynthia herself was starting to have doubts about it as she gave it a second look. 'Are you sure' she asked? Byron and Jenna nodded yes with the most positive looks they could muster. 'Well I'd best take it off for now, wouldn't want to crease it said Cynthia, who had planned to parade down stairs to show her family but changed her mind till she could feel better about it. So, she said as she came out of the closet a little disheartened but trying not to show it, have you picked out a dress yet Jenna.'

'Ah no, not yet I haven't had time' Jenna replied thinking that with a few touchups the cinderella dress would have to do but would be a far cry from the beauty of the exquisit violet gown that hung in Cynthias closet.

'Well let me know when you want to go said Cynthia I'll come with you.'

'Sounds great' said Jenna wondering what she would do about that. They spent another hour discussing places where Jenna and Byron could be seen together.

'This time said Cynthia when you say goodnight you have to hug longer, Byron was somber, or it won't look like your getting serious about each other.'

'Alright,' Jenna complied. Byron still looked a little nervous. Just think of me as your sister she added.

'Yes agreed Cynthia, the one you always wanted instead of the two you got.' They all laughed. Jenna arrived home later and later each night.


The next Saturday Cynthia and Byron showed up at the bakery. Cynthia stayed hidden in the car while Byron went into the bakery.

'Hello said Millie, Jenna is out in the kitchen, you can go right in.' O.k. said Byron as he walked out back. Jenna was up to her elbows in flour. 'Byron, she said in surprise, did I forget something?' 'No said Byron, Cynthia is in the car, her mother asked her to go to the mainland to pick up her dress for the Ball, it needed some, ah,

'Alterations' said Jenna.

'Yes that's it said Byron anyway we thought it might be a good chance for you to go dress shopping for your dress.'

'Oh, sighed Jenna about that . . .'

'Is something wrong' asked Byron?

'Ah no, said Jenna, but I won't need a fancy dress, remember I'm suppose to look poor.'

'But that's only till my mom accepts Cynthia over you and I was thinking of telling her before the Ball because your plan seems to be working so well, so I don't think you'll have to wear a poor dress after all, and you can use that money to buy any dress you like.'

'Oh didn't you hear said Millie who walked into the kitchen, Jenna gave the money away.' Byron looked shocked. Jenna quickly replied, 'One of my students has a brain tumour and neither his family nor this town had the eight hundred dollars, and they would need money for travel, and your father did say I could spend it anyway I wanted. I'll try and come up with something.'

Byron was in such shock he plopped down in a chair. 'You gave it all away?'

'Sorry said Jenna almost sarcastically but . . .'

'The whole thousand dollars???'

'I said I was sorry!

'Oh don't appologise said Byron it's the most amazing thing I've ever heard of and I'm going to make sure that the Christmas committee judges hear about this, I think it could score some points for your town, they are also looking for examples of unity within your own town.'

'But what about your town' asked Millie, don't you want it to win?

'No, said Byron, I don't care about the contest, this is what Christmas is all about, not sparkling trees. Mothers head of the committee this year and she's sparing no expense, there'll be twice as much tinsel and festival and hullabaloo, it gets so that you don't know what were celebrating anymore, I think it would do Richville good to lose for a change,

'Perhaps, said Jenna, but I didn't do this for points.'

'Of course you didn't said Byron as he hugged her, you wonderful angel you, wait till I tell Cynthia, oh I've got to go, she's waiting in the car, we'll talk later.'

Cynthia was moved to tears after hearing about Jenna. While they were waiting at the dress shop for the cleark to get the dress Cynthia noticed a black sparkly lacy dress that was so stunningly beautiful.

'Oh Byron look at this.' This just came in today said the sales clerk and with your long beautiful long red hair . . .'

'Why don't you try it on said Byron?'

'Right this way' said the clerk. She did look stunning in it. Again Cynthia was moved to tears. 'What do you think' she asked.

'Beautiful, amazing, I didn't want to hurt your feelings, said Byron, when you tried the other dress on, but I think this one looks ten times better on you.'

'Me too said Cynthia I think the other dress was the wrong color for me.'

'What color was it' asked the clerk?

'Light purple' answered Cynthia.

The clerk started to laugh then quickly covered her mouth. 'Oh please forgive me, who sold you that.'

'I got it at Annabellas,' answered Cynthia.

'Yes that doesn't surprise me said the clerk they will sell anything to anyone just to make a dollar. In this store we would not have let you walk out with a purple gown unless it was perhaps very dark purple, it simply is not your color.'

'The purple dress was beautiful said Cynthia it just didn't look beautiful on me once I got it home.'

No of course not, said the clerk, such a dress was made for someone with light brown hair, perhaps green eyes, hmm,

'JENNA,' cried Cynthia and Byron together.

'Does this Jenna have brown hair, green eyes, a bit darker complexion than yours asked the clerk.'

'YES,' exclaimed Cynthia and Byron at once.

'Then I agree said the clerk, a light purple dress would look very good on her.'

'And I will buy this one for you said Byron, an early Christmas present.'

'Oh I love you' cried Cynthia throwing her arms around him and plastering him with kisses.

'I love you too' laughed Byron. Cynthia quickly changed as Byron paid for the dress, she was so happy she even hugged the clerk.

'I can't wait to see Jenna said Cynthia. As soon as you drop me off . . .'

'I'll go and get her' said Byron.

He made up some excuse that Cynthia had some more plans for the ball.


By the time Jenna arrived to Cynthia's house, Cynthia had explained the whole thing to her parents and tried both dresses on for them and they loved the black one by far. It brought tears to her mother's eyes. Cynthia and her mother were waiting in Cynthia's room as Byron and Jenna entered.

'Oh my soul, said Jenna you're so beautiful, oh Cynthia that dress was made for you.'

'Thank you said Cynthia and this one was made for you' she announced as she opened the closet doors to reveal the violet dress.

'What' replied Jenna totally confused???

Cynthia explained how she saw the black dress when she went to pick up her mother's dress, and, how it looked so much better on her, and, how the clerk said the purple dress would look good on someone with Jenna's complexion, and, that they insisted on giving it to her as a Christmas present.

'Oh you can't, I couldn't,' disputed Jenna.

'Yes you can, said Cynthia, I insist, besides it's been altered; I can't take it back.'

Jenna just stood there with her mouth opened as though she were in shock.

'It's ok said Cynthia, you do so much for others; it's ok to let someone do something for you.'

'I, I never in my wildest dreams, I'll pay you back' said Jenna.

'No you won't,' Cynthia promptly disputed, 'but you will try it on right now, before you change your mind.'

Cynthia closed the doors to the closet and helped Jenna into her new dress; she also fixed up her hair and added a touch of makeup.

In a few minutes Cynthia opened the doors. Byron stood there alongside Cynthia's mother, with their mouths opened. It was as though Jenna and the dress were made for eachother.

'Amazing,' proclaimed Cynthia's mother. 'Absolutely, confirmed Byron, it's perfect.'

'And it fits perfect' said Cynthia. Jenna wanted to cry she never knew she could look like this. She wiped a tear.

'Oh don't cry, said Cynthia oh where's the tissues.

Oh where's those shoes that came with that dress,' Mrs Norris asked? 'That's right said Cynthia I won't need them now. I am never buying another purple dress she said as she handed Jenna the shoes.' The shoes were just a bit big.

'I can fix that said Mrs Norris, and she was back in a flash with insoles she put them in the shoes, there try that.'

'Perfect' said Jenna.

You look like an angel said Mrs Norris you both do. Thank you said Jenna thank you all so much. Your welcome dear said Mrs Norris as she left. Take the dress home and show Millie said Cynthia, if this doesn't give Jake a change of heart then he's totally heartless.

'Not to mention blind' added Byron.

Hey, scolded Cynthia, teasingly.

'Oh look at you, said Jenna, you've got nothing to worry about, it's Byron who'll have the problem keeping the other guys away from you.' Cynthia smiled as she twirled her dress in the mirror.

Millie thought the dress was the most beautiful thing she had ever seen and that Jenna did look like an angel in it.

'Jake will be amazed' she said. They would soon find out because the judging would be in a few days.

# Chapter Thirteen

## Jenna's Ring???

Ben, Jake, Matt and Tyler were almost finished with the tree. The houses were set in the tree but the mice would stay at the bakery till it was time to turn on the lights. The train worked really well starting at the top of the tree and winding around till it got to the bottom and then it went back up.

Ben and Jake built replicas of the train stations in the three villages, and the little train would pause at each station during its journey. They were thrilled about it and it looked like Pleasantville might actually have a chance of winning this year, but most of Pleasantville didn't know it. They wanted nothing to do with the tree. So it wasn't any problem to keep everything secret. Most of the people hadn't even planned on showing up for the judging.

Jenna was feeling a lot happier these days, 'hello Tyler' she said cheerfully as he came into the bakery but she was surprised to see him ignore her as he walked to the kitchen. 'What's wrong?' she asked as she entered behind him. 'You're not much help around here' he blurted out and Ben and Millie are too nice to say anything.' 'Excuse me?!!!?' 'That's not true said Millie, Jenna has been worked almost to exhaustion and you know it.' 'What's the real problem asked Jenna who was always quite good at reading her brother. He just scowled at her. I'ts alright she said you can say it, what ever it is.' 'I suppose you're going to marry that Byron now' he said with a look of discuss.

'Oh that's what it is' said Jenna smiling, you know Byron is wonderful, a really nice guy. Last night he put five hundred dollars in an envelope and left it on Billy's doorstep, we rang the door bell and ran away, then watched as they opened the envelope. Byron said it was the most fun he'd ever had and he would have to do it more often.'

'Yea said Tyler well I still say that Jake is better for you than he is.'

'So do I,' said Jenna. And so does Byron and his fiancée Cynthia.'

'What????' Tyler was totally confused.

'Tyler I have to admit that even with all your pranks and sneakiness, and marks that could be better; you have impressed me quite a lot lately. With everything that has gone on, with the mice the weasels, everything; you have shown more maturity than most boys your age.

That's why I'm going to trust you with the biggest secret ever.' Jenna told him the whole story. She knew Tyler would like the part about the snob sisters getting the dessert spilled all over them.

'That would have been something to see' he laughed.

'You must keep this a secret from Jake,' Jenna added.

'I promise' said Tyler hugging his sister.


'Well tomorrow is the big night said Millie I can hardly wait.'

'Yea said Tyler everything is all set and the mice are ready to move into their new home.'

'The mice, said Jenna, I haven't had time to spend with them lately, how are they doing?

'Great said Tyler they are as excited as we are. He noticed a sad look on Jenna's face. Whats wrong he asked.'

'Oh nothing said Jenna it's just that; if this really works they will be the unsung heroes of Pleasantville. We couldn't do this without them and no one will know.'

'True said Tyler but they wouldn't be here without us.'

'I suppose said Jenna. I just wish there was more we could do for them, some kind of reward.' 'Well said Millie why don't we see how they like their new clothes.'

'Oh I almost forgot about those said Jenna, do you suppose they'll still be awake?'

'I'll check' said Tyler.

'I'll get the clothes.'

'The Mice were really excited now with their beautiful little dresses and their smart looking suits and sweet little pointy hats. We thought you forgot about us said one little mouse, or didn't like us anymore said another, because we never saw you, Gregory told us you were busy, but now we know you were really, really, really busy.'

'I'm sorry said Jenna, I promise to spend more time with you I have really missed you little guys.'

'Hey look at you said Ben who just walked in, good job Jenna' he said patting her on the back. 'You all look so beautiful' said Millie with a tear.

'What's wrong' asked Gregory.

'It's just that when you're all living in the tree I'm really going to miss you.'

'But we'll be back said Gregory.' 'We promise said Oscar.'

'Didn't Gregory tell you said Ben, there's a tunnel that leads from the tree to here.'

'What' asked Millie in surprise?

'It's true said Gregory right through this door here.' He pointed to a little door in the wall.

'It originally went right under the bakery said Ben but we fixed it so that the mice could come back here in case it got stormy, or any time they want.'

'Wonderful' said Millie as she opened the little door.

'Well I just made the door said Ben the mice dug the tunnel and even put a string of spark lights to light the way.

'Perfect said Jenna, you can come back for supper.' 'And

we built extra houses to leave here,' added Ben. 'Oh that's wonderful said Millie, It's all coming together.'
'One step at a time' said Ben as he hugged her.

The next day there definitely was excitement in the air, at least at the bakery. The rest of the town seemed ho hum about the whole thing feeling certain that they were in for another embarrassing disappointment.
Byron came to pick up Jenna at around 4:00 pm.
'Byron your early said Jenna I thought we were leaving at six.'
'I know said Byron there's something I would like you to help me with first.'
'Sure said Jenna what is it.'
'Well, I'd like to pick out an engagement ring for Cynthia and I'd like your opinion.'
'Oh wow, said Jenna, does she know?'
She's not expecting it till after Christmas when things have died down and we had Mothers approval but I can't wait that long.'
'Well I really don't think Cynthia will mind' laughed Jenna. I'll just get changed and be right with you.'
Jenna put on her nicest outfit and hoped it would be good enough.

They soon arrived at Crystal Palace, the finest jewellery store in all of Richville. Jenna thought she walked into a magic land where the walls and ceilings glittered in gold, silver and crystals.
'I don't know where to start' said Byron.
'Wow I know what you mean, this place is incredible; why don't we split up said Jenna, we'll both pick something we think would suit her and then compare.'
'I guess that's as good a plan as any said Byron.

After searching for close to an hour they met at the counter by the window and showed each other their choice. Jenna laughed. 'What's so funny, said Byron I think mine looks good.'

'So do I, obviously said Jenna, as she held up her choice.'

'It's the same ring' declared Byron.

'I think it's the most beautiful ring here said Jenna.'

'Yes it is an excellent choice, said the attendant, our store is so big and so busy, that we order two of everything and put half on one side of the store and the other half on the other side. Still it is amazing that you both picked out the same style said the attendant, it shows you were made for each other.'

Before they could correct him . . .

'I don't think mother will agree,' came a sly voice from behind them. The snob sisters were snickering.

The attendant walked over to the counter not wanting to get in the middle of anything.

Byron was angry with them and wanted to straighten them out. 'It's not' . . . he began but Jenna nudged him hard in the ribs.

'It's just too bad about mother isn't it,' she snapped.

'OH,' the sisters gasped, 'you just wait till we tell her,' said Gertrude, dragging Henrietta away. 'Sorry if I hurt you Jenna apologised to Byron, but this was perfect, we couldn't have set it up any better if we tried, soon your mother will think we're engaged.' 'Your right said Byron Sometimes I just get so mad at them I can't think straight.

'Common said Jenna linking his arm with her's, let's go get your ring.' They walked over to the counter and the attendant set both rings on the counter. Jenna happened to look up and in a large mirror on the wall she saw a reflection of the snob sisters peeking behind the counter. She nudged Byron again, only lighter this time and with her eyes, motioned for him to look in the mirror, he could see them too as a smile came across his face.

'Shall we try it on,' asked the attendant?'

'Absolutely' said Byron. 'As you wish said the attendant as he handed Byron the box. Byron took the ring and slid it on Jenna's finger.

'Oh my, she said, it's exquisite.'

'You have lovely hands,' said the attendant, and the ring sits like a crown on your lovely hands.'

'I think its perfect, said Byron, in fact I don't want you to take it off, and then he gave Jenna a smile.

'Oh darling' she said as she hugged him and kissed his cheek almost giggling. They looked up to the mirror and saw Byron's sisters rushing out the door in a look of shock.

'We'll take it' said Byron to the attendant.

'I'll get the papers' the accountant replied.

'I can't wait to tell Cynthia' said Byron.

'I wish she could have been here just to see the look on your sister's faces,' laughed Jenna.

'Let's tell her tonight' said Byron.

'About the ring asked Jenna, aren't you keeping it a surprise for a few days?'

'I guess I should' said Byron.

Jenna wore the ring out to the car but before they drove off she took it off her finger and gave it to Byron who put it in the velvet box. A few minutes later they arrived at Cynthia's house, her mother answered the door. 'Am I ever glad to see you both here,' she stressed as she hurried them in.

'What's wrong' asked Jenna?

'It's Cynthia, she's up in her room crying and won't speak to anyone, replied Mrs Norris.' They rushed upstairs Byron knocked on the door, 'Cynthia what's wrong can we come in.'

The door opened, Cynthia walked back to her bed. Byron rushed to her and grabbed her by the arms, what happened?!!!? Did someone hurt you??? Cynthia closed her eyes tight as more tears fell down her cheeks, how could he ask that, she thought. She nodded.

Who!!!' demanded Byron?

'You' whispered Cynthia.

'What???Byron, Jenna, and Cynthia's mother looked at each other confused, how???'

'I don't blame you said Cynthia, either one of you, I pretty much threw you together, I understand.

'Well I'm glad you do cause I sure don't' said Byron backing away and getting frustrated. Cynthia started to cry again and her mother hugged her. 'I, I, . . . I saw you tonight she sniffed, at the Crystal Palace.'

'You were there?' asked Jenna, this was all starting to make sense to her.

Cynthia nodded 'Father sent me to pick up a Christmas present for Mom.'

'He did?' asked her mom.

Cynthia nodded, 'but like I said I don't blame you.'

'Well good said Byron cause there's nothing to blame!'

Now Cynthia looked confused and a little hurt, Jenna thought shed better clear this up.

'Cynthia, you didn't see Byron's sisters there did you?'

She slowly shook her head no.

Jenna looked at Byron, 'She must have come in right after they left, I'm sorry but we have to tell her everything.' He nodded in agreement.

'Cynthia, Byron came over to my house early because he wanted me to go with him, to Crystal Palace, to help him pick out an' . . . she looked at Byron again,

'An engagement ring said Cynthia I know I saw' she said sniffing.'

'Yes said Jenna but the ring was for you, not me, it was going to be a surprise and while we were looking at the one Byron chose, his sisters came up behind us thinking the ring was for me and threatened to tell mother. So we played along hoping they would tell Mother, that way she would welcome you with open arms when Byron told her the truth. We thought they might be still watching us so I kept the ring on and we kept our act up till we got in the car. We couldn't wait to get here to tell you, honest said Jenna as she held up her hand, see, no ring, you do believe me don't you?'

Tears rolled down Cynthia's cheeks again. I'm even more stupid than your dumb sisters she cried into her hands, I'm so sorry.'

'We were really convincing said Jenna, putting an arm around her, even the store clerk believed us, didn't he Byron.'

Byron was looking away, feeling hurt that she would doubt his love and loyalty for her.

'We were convincing' Jenna repeated to him!

'I'm so sorry I doubted you, both of you she cried, can you ever forgive me?'

Byron smiled a little, her tears softened his heart. 'No one's as stupid as my dumb sisters he said. I love Jenna, Jenna looked shocked worrying that she may have over played her role, she's brilliant he continued, she's like the sister I always wanted instead of the two idiots I got, and I will hold her a dear friend forever, Jenna was touched by his words, but you, . . .' he took the little box out of his pocket and handed it to her.

'Oh I don't deserve this' she said.

'No said Byron getting down on one knee and opening the box, you deserve better, but would you do me the honor of marrying me anyway.' Cynthia fell into his arms crying and Jenna and Mrs. Norris, also in tears, left the room.

A few minutes later Byron and Cynthia came down stairs all smiles and Cynthia went straight to Jenna and hugged her tightly. 'I'm so sorry' she said.

'Don't be silly' said Jenna, it only means that we played our roles well and Byron's mother will be only too happy to accept you over poor little ol me,' she laughed.

'Byron's mother should be happy said Mrs. Norris giving Cynthia a hug, now about that gift your father sent for ...'

'Oh said Cynthia, I didn't get it and I swear I don't know what it is, he just said they'd have it ready.'

'We can go get it now said Byron, on our way to the tree judging.'

'It can wait for tomorrow said Mrs Norris I'm sure Crystal Palace has closed early for the judging.'

'Oh yea that's right said Byron.'

'Besides, said Cynthia is't almost time to leave.'

'Oh this is exciting' said Mrs Norris just then they heard a car horn in the yard. 'Oh theres your father time to go', everyone hurried to get their coats on. It rarely snowed on the island except for high on the mountain, but it did get a little chilly in the winter.

'Oh before we go, said Cynthia as she took off her ring,' here she said as she gave it to Jenna, you have to wear this for tonight.'

Jenna smiled, 'good idea, we'll make sure Byron's mother sees it.' Cynthia giggled, she went with her parents and Jenna went with Byron. As they drove to Richville, [because the contest always starts in Richville,] Jenna was quietly looking at the ring on her finger. 'You all right' asked Byron?

'Just wondering if Jake will ever place a ring on my finger, answered Jenna.

'We'll do everything we can to make sure he does' said Byron.

'I've decided that if this doesn't work with Jake, I'm leaving, to the mainland, I can't be around him anymore and pretend we're just friends, when I feel so much more for him and I'm clueless as to what he feels. I don't even think he cares. I've received word from a couple of schools on the mainland who are willing to hire me in the new year, but I want you to know that weather this works or not I will always be greatful for my two best friends.'

Byron didn't know what to say, he had to hold back a tear, but was more determined than ever to make this work. 'It will work he said, it has to.'

## Chapter Fourteen

# Oh Christmas Tree Oh Christmas Tree

Once they arrived they went to sit with Byron's family in the stand. Gertrude and Henrietta politely said hello but it was only to please their father and to check out if Jenna had a ring on her finger, which they straight way went and reported to mother. Mrs Edwards's heart pounded heavy and she avoided Byron and Jenna for fear she might explode or cry. This was an important night for her family and for Richville and she wasn't going to make a scene.

Now that the family was all together and the judges were there on the Mayor's stand, Mayor Edwards wasted no time introducing Jenna to the judges as he before hand mentioned their plan for unity. And Jenna carried on how greatful she was for for the invitation and what a great idea she thought it was, she also boasted about how Mayor Edwards provided toys for all the children at the school in Pleasantville and how excited the children were.

Mayor Edwards was pleasantly surprised as he didn't expect that and he gave Jenna a warm smile.

'Welcome, welcome everyone began Mayor Edwards, and thank you all for coming to our tree lighting ceremony, a special welcome to our honourable judges, sitting here on the stand.' Everyone clapped and cheered wanting the judges to feel special.

'Before we light the tree Iwould especially like to thank everyone on the Christmas tree committee. I feel it only right to introduce to you those talented individuals who worked tirelessly to make this night a spectacular one for you.

Tree committee, if you will come up here when your names are called we would like to present you with a token of our appreciation.

Adrienne Dixon

Robert Bannister

Heidi Mackillop

Terrence Wheeler

Alfred Dykeman

Joanne Rowe, and of course my wonderful wife and head of the committee Lydia Edwards.'

Everyone cheered as each of the names were called and went up to receive a nice gift basket then everything went silent.

First there was a low rumbling noise which grew louder, it was a drum roll and then a symphony began to play and each time the drum beat heavy, lights lit up on the tree and the crowd cheered. More and more lights, it seemed like it would never end. The people were amazed, it really was spectacular.

Finally there was one single horn left playing, by a man standing in front of the tree and as he hit the last high note the huge star at the top of the tree lit up. Everyone was just in awe, some were even crying, and then it was silent, but only for a moment till they saw the most incredible fireworks display ever, oh what joy filled their hearts. They had quickly forgotten about the cold, slightly breezy night. And as if that wasn't enough there was a troop of people dressed in elf costumes going out through the crowd handing out bags of candy, and thank you cards to each person. Jenna thought that Richville really went all out but she found that she absolutely loved it. She hadn't been to their lighting ceremony since she was a little girl, always too busy at the bakery this time of year. Then she thought about what Pleasantville had in store for the people and wondered how well they would do. It certainly wouldn't be this noisy. She feared it might not get as great a reaction.

Next they were off to Midville, where they were grateful to find the festivities inside the Grand Hall as it was getting rather chilli.

The hall was a huge two story building lavishly decorated and it easily fit everyone inside. The second floor was mainly balcony all around and opened in the middle so everyone could see down to the first floor.

In the center of the hall stood a large tree almost as big as Richville, it reached up pass the second story, but it was not yet lit up.

It was all beautifully decorated and had many, round tables set for four guests with a nice tray of yummy treats and a cup of hot cocoa waiting to warm each person.

As each person came in they were handed a program with a candy cane and directed to their seats. Many chose to sit upstairs as it did have a nice view. A special stand was built for the honoured guests; the Mayor's of Richville and Pleasantville, their families and of course the Govenor of mainland and his judges.

Christmas music was playing in the back ground and everyone was really grateful to be out of the cold and into such a warm cosy reception. Mayor Edwards and his wife, who were sure nothing could compare to Richvilles festivities, were starting to be a little concerned. They wished they had invited the other Mayors on their stand, not just the judges, and they noticed that everyone was already excited and the festivities hadn't even started yet.

Mayor Henderson welcomed everyone and said how greatful he was that they could come. He said they had never seen the hall so full and that on New Years Eve there would be a big dance held and that they had hired a popular band from the main land, everyone was welcome. Cheers rang out at that announcement.

Midvilles Grand Hall was the biggest hall on the island and built to attract people from everywhere, which it often did. Many would be buying their tickets for the New Year's dance before they left that night.

Thank you again for coming, he said, special thanks to all who worked tirelessly for this special night, and let the festivities begin.

The lights dimmed a little, and a choir began to sing, they sounded like angels, and the tree began to light up. It was beautiful, there were no fireworks of course, as they were inside, but as the choir hit their last note, the large star at the top of the tree lit up and many of the ornaments on the tree spun around. All the lights went out except for those on the dazzling tree, and there was silence for a few moments as everyone stared at the tree in amazement. After a few moments the lights came on and everyone was treated to a few short plays about Christmas and how it brings unity one was quite funny. Even the Edwards found themselves laughing.

There was also a choir of little children, dressed as angels; they were so sweet it just melted everyone's heart.

Again Jenna wondered about Pleasantville, they didn't have anything like this, there were no choirs, Christmas plays, angel costumes, perhaps they would not win this year but she knew at least they would not be forgotten. She was certain that everyone would like the lights and the little houses and the mice who had practised hard for their part to act like toy mice. Jenna thought of all the hard work they did and couldn't help feeling a tinge of guilt about leaving everyone behind to get set up while she enjoyed such spectacular displays. She couldn't dwell on that because it was now time to leave. Mayor Edwards turned to his daughters who had been unusually quiet and on their best behaviour, which made him a little nervous. This was the moment that they usually whined about wanting to go home, but this year he would not put up with that. 'Now girls it's time to carry on to Pleasantville.' 'O.K. Daddy' they happily answered making him even more nervous, but at least they weren't making a scene.

# Chapter Fifteen

## Magical

As everyone approached Pleasantville, everything was dark. It looked deserted; then, a tree appeared all lit up. And underneath it stood Jake directing the traffic to park off to the right in the big field behind the fish market. Once the group was gathered by the lit tree Jake could see that there were not very many there. Jenna could also see that most of the crowd at the other two villages opted not to come as they probably thought it was a waste of time and would put a damper on their spectacular evening thus far.

'So is this your tree Jake,' snickered one nasty fella from the audience? Some of the others laughed. Jake didn't answer; he noticed Jenna and Byron with his arm around her, and turned away.

'If you will all follow me' he said as he walked off into the dark.

Everyone stood still, thinking this was really strange, no one could see Jake anymore; some were about ready to turn around and walk away, thinking that Jake had played some terrible trick on them, but the judges and the Mayors led the way.

As they took a few steps, suddenly a tree on each side of them lit up beautifully, as though they caused it to light up. 'Wow,' 'amazing,' came the replies from the crowd. The trees continued to light up on each side of the street with each step. Two by two, they lit up as the enchanted spectators walked past them. The people were bewildered. They had never seen so many lights, not even in Richville.

'Shh said one man, listen.'

As everyone quieted down they could hear hundreds of tiny little bells.

Jenna had forgotten about those, Ben picked them up on the mainland and had the mice string them through the trees. As they continued on in silence, everyone noticed that they were cosy warm though it was getting even colder outside. Jenna could plainly see that they were just as amazed here as they were at the other two villages. Although their festivities were spectacular, this was like . . . magic.

Jenna already knew the plan, but she had to admit she was quite impressed herself.

Everyone gathered around the Christmas tree where Millie, Ben and the boys were waiting. When all were assembled, Ben stepped up on a little stand, beside the tree, to address the crowd. 'Hello, hello, he said in a jolly tone, and welcome, everyone to our Pleasantville Christmas. All aboard the Christmas Train for a wonderful tour around the island.'

Just as he said that the tree lit up, on cue glittering brilliantly, which drew oohs and ahh's from the crowd. The fact that every light on the tree was white, made the tree glow from the inside out, different from the other two trees with their many coloured lights, no one had ever had a tree with all white lights before, and the once empty spaces between the branches now held the charming little houses with adorable little waving mice. All of it made the tree seemed to come alive. Again it left everyone with that feeling of magic.

Then they heard a train whistle and saw, at the bottom of the tree a beautifully decorated train and in the head car they saw a tiny conductor. 'A-ll a-boa-rd' said Gregory in his best robotic voice. Everyone thought he was so cute, no one guessed he was real. They all followed Ben as he took them on a tour around the tree through the three villages, ending at the top in Richville, then heading down again.

Every time the train passed a house or building, a tiny mouse would come out and wave.

'Oh look said one lady from Midville, there's my flower shop.'

'And there's my restaurant' said a man from Richville. Many of the people's houses, and all three of the town halls were there.

Mayor Edwards noticed how the judges looked on in amazement; they seemed to have an excitement about them that they didn't have in Richville or Midville, almost childlike. Mayor Edwards thought that after the other two dazzling displays, Pleasantville would pale in comparison, as usual but there was something different about this, it seemed . . . well I guess there's just no other word for it, . . . magical.

While the other displays were really eye popping, this one went straight to everyone's heart, including his own.

When the train reached the bottom for the second time it paused for a moment as Ben stood back on his stand. 'Thank you for joining us on our little journey. And now, as you know, no Christmas tree is ever really complete without . . .' he removed a veil revealing the beautiful large nativity scene all lit up and the beautiful angels that Matt's mom was hiding. At first she froze as everyone around her clapped and cheered, thinking that her husband found out, and this was his doing. As she looked at him, she saw that he was cheering right along.

Then Ben spoke again, 'a special thanks goes to Mrs. Flossie McGregor our mayor's wife for this wonderful donation to our Christmas scene.'

Mrs McGregor, still frozen, didn't know what to say. 'Flossie, said the mayor to his wife, what a marvellous idea' he said as he gave her a big hug. Mrs McGregor then realised he knew nothing about it.

'You, you don't mind do you' she said?

'Mind, said Mayor, this is the best Christmas present I could ever have, I wanted to do something for the town to lift their spirits and give them hope and I was at a loss for ideas. But you have gone ahead and done it for me and kept it as a surprise too. Now the people can't help but have hope as they look at your beautiful display.'

As Mrs McGregor listened to her husband she realised how important his job was to him, and his great love for the people of this town and it brought tears to her eyes as she vowed in her heart to help him more and be less concerned with appearances.

You're amazing he said as he gave her another hug and a kiss on the cheek. Then she realised that if this wasn't his doing . . . she looked to Matt who was standing with Ben Tyler and Jake. He looked back at her with a sheepish grin on his face. She realised that in all the hustle and bustle she had actually seen very little of him and also vowed to spend more time with him as well. She would even find that list he gave her and buy him everything on it. His act of charity taught her the real meaning of Christmas, and renewed her love for her family. She returned to him a big smile and a wink, and mouthed the words, thank you.

'Looks like your Christmas is saved after all' said Ben in a low tone. Matt smiled with excitement.

'And now said Ben if you'll follow me this way to the reception hall, we have refreshments for you.'

As everyone followed Ben, Mrs McGregor grabbed her son and gave him a big hug. But most of the people just grabbed one of the benches that circled the Christmas tree to watch the train and admire the houses and lights and mice, or they sat on one of the many benches under the other brightly lit trees in the warm cosy atmosphere given off by the lights, sipping punch and going on about how marvellous everything was. Although the hall was nicely decorated very few even entered it or if they did it was only to grab a few snacks then back out to admire the tree.

It looked, to Jenna as though all their hard work finally payed off, it didn't even matter that only half of the crowed that attended Richville and Midville's displays, carried on to Pleasantville, in fact it seemed a blessing, because it wouldn't have been so enchanting with the whole crowd of noisy people.

Gertrude and Henrietta also found something they admired; though it had nothing to do with Christmas, it was the reason for their unusual good behaviour. They believed that Jenna was the only thing keeping him, from them, so they told him all about seeing her and Byron at Crystal Palace Jewlers and the ring they picked out. It was obvious that Jake was confused. He never thought Jenna would be so hasty, so rash.

'If you don't believe us said Gertrude have a look for yourself.' Jake felt as though his legs were jelly, and his heart was raceing, but he turned and walked back to the tree. And there he saw it with his own eyes. Jenna was giving Molly a hug, in all the excitement, and there on Jenna's finger was a beautiful diamond ring. He was grateful they didn't see him.

Poor Jake was feeling so good, their Christmas plans had gone off like clockwork. He was on cloud nine over the impressive comments from everyone, even the Mayors and the judges, all of the hard work really paid off, and now, suddenly, . . . none of it mattered anymore, his heart was broken and he just wanted to dig a hole and bury himself. He snuck away and went home. The snob sisters who were watching all of this thought that by the time Jake reached home he'd have enough time to get over this or perhaps they could help him so he'd feel better by tomorrow of course they had never been in love but Jake had been in love, with Jenna, all of his life. He walked extra fast so that he was home five minutes before Gertrude and Henrietta reached his house. They knocked on the door, and thinking it might be Ben or by the remotest possibility it might be Jenna, he hurried to the door, but when he opened it and saw the snob sisters there, that was the last straw. He had had more than enough and was through being nice to them.

'Hello Jake said Gertrude are you o.k. we . . . .'

BANG went the door in their faces making them both jump. The two stunned girls stood there staring at the door hardly believing what just happened as they heard him lock the door from the other side.

Henrietta looked to Gertrude, 'I think he might need just a little bit more time,' she said.

Gertrude whacked Henrietta, 'common!

'Where have you been,' asked their father suspiciously when they returned?

'Oh Henrietta wanted to look at every tree, said Gertrude, I don't know why, they're all the same.'

Henrietta was about to protest but Gertrude whacked her again, 'can we go home now' she added. Mayer Edward's thought it best not to try their patience any longer.

Byron walked Jenna to her house. 'Well I must say you've given Richville a run for its money.' 'We didn't have fireworks' replied Jenna.

'You didn't need them' said Byron.

'I'm glad you enjoyed it said Jenna as they reached her front door. They both looked at the tool Barn.

'Do you suppose he's watching' asked Byron?

'He's probably back at the celebration said Jenna, I saw your sisters corner him.'

'Yes said Byron and I saw him hastily leave shortly after, he looked upset, I know he doesn't like them but can't imagine what they said to upset him that much.'

'Oh, my guess is that they told him about the ring said, Jenna.

Jenna gasped, the ring I forgot I had it on' she began to remove it but Byron stopped her hands. 'I think you'd better keep it on for now said Byron, we wouldn't want him spotting you without it, Ill explain to Cynthia; she'll be thrilled.' Jenna gave him a hug and she went inside.

Jake had never been so angry, and he wasn't really angry at the snob sisters, he was more angry at himself for not finding the courage to ask Jenna out sooner. He didn't expect her to wait forever but he didn't know it would feel like this when someone else asked her to marry him. And he really couldn't blame anyone else for wanting to marry her, he only blamed himself. He knew what he had to do, after Christmas was over he would leave his store to Ben and leave for the Mainland, find a way to start all over again, no one needed him here and he couldn't stand to see Jenna with someone else any longer. It was the only choice he had.

## Chapter Sixteen

——✿——

# And The Winner Is

The next evening everyone gathered at the Midville dance hall for the judge's announcement. Jake didn't care who won any more, he didn't even want to go but Ben wouldn't let him miss it. Jake felt so out of place with all the excitement around him, that life was going on without him. He had some rough Christmases as a kid but this one beat them all. The Mayors and their families were on the stands as they were the night before. There was Jenna looking very happy with Byron's arm around her again. The one good thing about this whole situation, Jake thought was that Byron was a good guy. Jake got to know him a little from working for his father and they got along really well. Yes Jenna would be happy with him and well cared for.

'And now" came the announcer, for the moment you have all waiting for . . . the judges stepped up to their microphones, may I introduce to you our honoured judges Mr. David Radcliff, Mrs Evelyn Watson and Mr. Richard Grint,' cheers rang out as the announcer returned to his seat as the judges approached the stand. Mr. Radcliff was the first to speak. 'First of all congratulations on a fantastic display all of you, well done well done.' Everyone cheered. 'Yes, added Mrs Watson you certainly made our job very difficult.' Cheers continued. 'We appreciate the tremendous amount of hard work that went into each display said Mr Grint. More cheers. We'll begin by each telling you what we liked about each display and we'll start with Richville.' Everyone from Richville cheered, but Mayor Edwards had an uneasy feeling that they were saving the best for last.

'Fantastic tree, said Mr Grint, and incredible fireworks. The music building up to the fireworks fit just perfect and was wonderful. The costumed elves were the perfect finishing touch. Well done Richville.' Again everyone cheered. Jenna felt a little guilty cheering so she only cheered a little, only because she was on the stand.

Next, said Mrs Watson is Midville. Cheers rang again. The wonderful refreshments that greeted us were very much appreciated by all. The hall was elegantly decorated and the tree was amazing. It was so nice to be warm and cozy so we could relax and enjoy the sweet entertainment put on by the children that just warmed everyones heart. Well done Midville.' Cheers rang out once more.

'And last said Mr Radcliff, but certainly not least is Pleasantville. This time everyone cheered even those from Richville and Midville which surprised those from Pleasantville. The Pleasantville experience was totally unexpected said Mr Radcliff and completely different from the other two towns. In fact it was completely different from anything we had ever seen, ever.

To begin with the silent walk in the dark, as our footsteps seemed to cause a magnificent canopy of tiny lights, to appear above us, while the tinkling sound of tiny bells filled the air.

It was, to use a word that seemed most popular last night . . . magical.

It put us all in a state of awe, and, at a loss for words, hence, the silent walk.

And then there was the tree, certainly one of a kind. I can honestly say I've never seen a tree with a train in it. And the decorations were very nice.

And although we were outside the lights seemed to keep us warm, but if we chose to we could also go into the hall to sit and enjoy a tasty treat.

Well done Pleasantville.'

Everyone cheered again but many thought, especially Milly that he could have said more about the decorations. After all their hard work, hours and hours, and he didn't even mention the mice and their sweet little costumes.

The prize this year said Mr Radcliff of one hundred thousand dollars, goes to the town who we feel most embodied the spirit of Christmas.'

'Yes continued Mrs Watson, it was a very hard decision in deed each town was so amazing and thrilling but the town we chose showed us the true meaning of unity.'

'In deed added Mr Grint, this year's winner showed their love for all by including all three villages in their presentation in a very ingenious way. And the winner is . . .' he looked to Mrs Watson who, with a big smile on her face and tears welling up in her eyes, announced,

'PLEASANTVILLE!!!'

Cheers suddenly roared so loud from all three villages that they could probably be heard from the mainland. Millie was in shock, with tears streaming down her face. Ben held on to her tightly. He and the others were so thrilled, even Jake was caught up in the moment; at least he was until he saw Byron give Jenna a congratulatory hug, and then he remembered his broken heart.

Mr Radcliff spoke again. 'Though the theme for this year's contest is Unity at Christmas, and although many good deeds have been reported to us, in the end it was decided that we were sent here to judge the trees only, and we feel that the Pleasantville tree, A Trip Around the Island was indeed most astonishing. It resembled the true meaning of Christmas and of unity by including everyone in their tree.'

'We noticed said Mr Grint how everyones face lit up as they saw a replica of their own houses or buildings in the Pleasantville tree. And to have a train go around the tree from top to bottom was an ingenious idea and must have taken a great deal of work to fortify those branches,' Ben, was smiling from ear to ear.

'The houses were remarkable said Mrs Watson and the mice with their adorable little costumes were just precious.'
[You don't know how precious, thought Millie with more tears.]
'It is now time to present the award so Mayor McGregor would you please come forward.'
Mayor McGregor took the stand. He wasn't quite prepared for this.
'Thank you thank you' he said as the cheers died down. 'First of all I must thank all of you for your support, your cheers have warmed our hearts and has been greatly appreciated.' More cheers rang out. 'And I also want to thank the Judges, [more cheers rang out,] for all the work they have done. For their kind words, for being able to see and understand all the detail and tremendous work that went into each of our town's trees and helping us all to appreciate them even more. I certainly would not have wanted to be in their position. Let's have another round of applause for the judges shall we . . . but most of all, most of all, there are six people in particular who are responsible for our success. They were the only ones who really believed in the project and worked tirelessly to make it a reality. So if you would please come up here, Ben and Millie Hopkins, Jake Anderson, Jenna Hopkins, Tyler Hopkins, and . . . he kind of choked a little with pride . . . my son Matt McGregor.'
Again loud cheers rang out as they made their way across the stage. Mayor McGregor passed the microphone to Jake who quickly passed it to Ben as his heart just wasn't in it anymore and he didn't think he could fake it; acting as excited as the rest of them were. His world was falling apart; every chance for happiness was disappearing right before his eyes.

'Well first of all began Ben, we would also like to thank everyone for their tremendous support, it, . . . well it means a great deal to us, and we'll never forget it. I want to thank my family here and friends who worked so hard . . . Ben began to tear up . . . for this. He was anxious to get off stage. 'Thank you all and MERRY CHRISTMAS.'

The cheers rang out louder than ever and almost blew the roof off. Mayor McGregor took the mike again. 'Thank you once again, I'd like to invite you all to our Christmas ball tomorrow night. There will be much to do for it because no one believed we would win, no one but these wonderful people, he said, and so no preparations were made, but one thing's for sure, this wonderful bunch, he said pointing to Ben and his crew will not be called on, they will have a well-deserved day of rest, and the rest of our town will be pitching in. We look forward to seeing you all.' Jake left the celebration early and disappeared before anyone knew he was gone. He just didn't feel like pretending to be happy when none of this really mattered to him any more. Indeed it was a Merry Christmas, for everyone except him.

Byron's mother was also having a rough night. She didn't know what troubled her more, the fact that they lost the Christmas tree contest, [as head of the committee she continually bragged and boasted on her ideas,] or was it the sight of her only son standing arm in arm with an ignorant, money seeking, girl from PEASANTVILLE! All in all it was just a terribly upsetting and depressing night for her. When Byron returned home he heard something coming from the study. He opened the door to find his mother in tears and his father standing hopelessly beside her who was relieved to see Byron and invited him in. Byron asked 'what's wrong?'

'Everything! His mother replied. First we lost the Christmas tree contest, I had never been head of the committee but I promised them if they voted for me we'd surely win and it's the first year we've lost. I went way beyond our budget, I even bought out all the left over tree lights on the mainland just to make sure no one's tree would shine as bright as ours, she sobbed, and not only did we lose, we lost to, to, to POORVILLE! But I could get over all that she said wiping her nose, it's just that now my son, my only son wants to marry a, a, a . . .'

'Jenna is a lovely girl' claimed Byron.

'Yes of course son but she's just after your money replied his mother with a few more tears and we'll be the laughing stock of the island.' She sobbed harder, Byron laughed,' if only you knew how little she cares about money.' His mother shook her head as though she didn't believe him, and he knew he wouldn't win that argument but something told him that now was the time to tell her the truth.

'You worry too much about what people think said Byron.'

'You sound like your father she replied.'

'Well that's good, said Byron he's a smart man, and like him I don't care what people think, but I'm not going to marry Jenna.'

'What' sniffed Mrs. Edwards?

'That's right said Byron, Jenna and I are not getting married, what gave you that idea,' he asked knowing perfectly well.

'Your sisters' she said.

'You know how they are mom, he replied, always making up stories, do you know they sneak off to Pleasantville every chance they get to visit Jake, he wants nothing to do with them of course.' 'Oh wait till I get my hands on them' snapped Mrs Edwards.

'But Mom,' continued Byron as he took a deep breath, 'there is someone, that I love, and I do want to marry her, and I will marry her, but she's not from Richville.'

'Ohhh, sighed his mom, is she from Pleasantville too?'

'No said Byron, she's from Midville.'

'Really,' said Mrs. Edwards brightening up.

'Yes' said Byron surprised at the sudden enlightened tone of her voice, but deciding to remain firm . . . 'and I know you never wanted us to marry out of Richville, but' . . .

'I was wrong about that said his mother, I want you to marry whomever you love, I, I just want you to be happy, you did say she's from Midville? She asked making sure it wasn't Pleasantville? Byron smiled, 'yes' he said showing her a picture from his wallet.

'Cynthia Norris!???' His mom was surprised.

'You know her asked Byron? She didn't mention it.'

'She doesn't know replied his mom but the hospital board has asked your father to invite Cynthia to work in the Richville hospital, she has excellent credentials and they felt that if she were asked by the Mayor . . . and he asked me to come along, says I'm good at persuasion, imagine. We were going to do it after Christmas, she's the best in her field of physiotherapy and they are in desperate need.' 'But now that she's going to marry you, said Mayor Edwards putting in his stamp of approval, she won't need a job will she.'

'Oh that won't stop her,' said Byron, she's the best at what she does because she loves her work. So your o.k. with this he added?'

'Absolutely' said Mrs Edwards as she reached for her son's hand. 'And I wish you both, every happiness.' 'Oh we must have Cynthia and her family over for dinner, she said as she hugged her son, this is turning out to be a pretty good Christmas after all, and I'm sorry she said turning to her husband, about all the money I wasted on the Christmas project, the council didn't mention it but I'm sure they want to kill me.'

'It wasn't a waste said the Mayor, it was a wonderful display that brought delight to all, and about the budget', his wife looked a little worried, 'the council didn't mention it because, well I didn't tell you because, I know how you can um, over do things sometimes, but we actually had a bigger budget than what I told you,' his wife now looked pleasantly surprised, 'you actually came under by three dollars and fifty eight cents.'

'Oh this is a great Christmas after all' said Lydia as she pulled her husband and son into a group hug.

# Chapter Seventeen

—*෨෨*—
# Nothing Short Of A Miracle

The next day the bakery shop was closed and everyone slept in. Later, Ben, Tyler and Matt tended to the mice. Jenna did some tidying and Millie baked a special celebration dinner. Jake didn't come over at all. By five thirty Ben had, had enough and decided to drag Jake over if he had to, which he just about did.

'Have a seat said Millie, suppers ready.'

Jenna had set up a special table, nicely decorated for everyone. She came out from the kitchen with a basket of rolls and suddenly stopped briefly when she saw Jake sitting at the table. Their eyes met for a brief second as she set the rolls down she noticed his eyes fell upon the ring on her finger.

He wanted so badly to get up and walk out and never come back, somehow, for the first time ever, he didn't feel like he belonged there anymore.

Just then a knock came at the door. 'I'll get it' said Millie. Cynthia bursted through the door with Byron following, 'it worked it worked Jenna.'

'What' asked Jenna?

'Your brilliant plan, Byron, you explain,' insisted Cynthia.

'O. K. said Byron as he went on to relate the details of the night before.

'And that's pretty much how it went' said Byron.

'Actually, said Cynthia we just came from that dinner at his place, and it went very well.'

'Yea said Byron and guess who got stuck doing the dishes, and they have to miss the ball tonight to polish the silver, I almost feel sorry for them, almost,' he laughed.

Everyone joined in except for Jake who was stunned at what he heard; Byron and Cynthia didn't see him sitting in the corner.

'Well, I guess you'd better do this right said Jenna, taking the ring off her finger and handing it to Byron, I'm so glad it worked.'

'Me too said Byron as he got down on one knee. Cynthia you are the most amazing person Iv'e ever met and my life would be empty without you, with or without mothers approval I would have asked this anyway, will you marry me.'

'Yes of course' cried Cynthia as she hugged him. Millie wiped a tear while everyone else smiled, everyone but Jake. As everyone was congratulating the happy couple, Jake slipped out the door.


So this was all a ploy to get Byron's mother to agree to the marriage, he was almost happy for them, but he couldn't shake the feeling that a trick had been played on him as well. They were quite convincing even when no one was around them he thought. As he entered his front door he still didn't know what to think.

'Where did Jake go' asked Millie who was the first to notice his absence. 'Jake was here' asked Cynthia?

'I think he went home' said Tyler.

Jenna looked a bit upset thinking now that he knows the truth he still wants nothing to do with her.

'I'm sure the poor guy's in shock said Cynthia and needs a little time to sort out his feelings.'

'I think I'll pay him a visit and help him to sort them out' said Byron.

'Perfect said Cynthia and we can get ready, I brought my stuff.'

'Oh great said Jenna, let's bring it upstairs.'

The girls brought Cynthia's stuff upstairs, and Byron went over to Jakes. Tyler ran to catch up with him, 'do you mind if I come' he asked?

'No said Byron, you know Jake better than I do.'

Byron was about to knock on Jakes door but Tyler just opened it and walked in. 'Hey Jake, he said, you here?' Jake entered the front shop and turned the lights on.

'Tyler? Byron, he said in surprise, ah, congratulations' he said shaking Byron's hand.

'Thank you said Byron, none of it would have been possible without Jenna, it was all her idea. You should have seen the act she put on for my mother acting like a poor ignorant little girl, she was hilarious.'

Jake couldn't imagine that. 'I thought, he said that you two, . . . I mean your sisters said . . ;'

'I know said Byron, they were spying on us so we had to make it look good . . . but . . . my mother is not the only reason we did this.'

'She isn't?'

'No said Byron, there was someone else we had to fool.'

'There was asked Jake, who?'

'You' answered Byron.

'Why, asked Jake after a few silent seconds. What did I do?'

'It's what you didn't do Jake and it hurt her deeply. Jenna has become one of my best friends and I care about her very much, she is a remarkable woman.'

'Yes she is said Jake, and she deserves better than me.'

'Perhaps, said Byron but she wants you. You have to let the past go Jake because from what I hear about you you're a pretty remarkable fella yourself; Jenna see's that and if you give her a chance, she'll help you see it too. Well I'd better get back, hope to see you there tonight.'

'I gotta go too said Tyler Millie'll have a fit if I don't get dressed up proper, but I just wanna say one thing.'

'What's that' asked Jake?

'Everyone thinks you're pretty smart Jake, some say your the smartest guy on the island, and definitely Pleasantville. But if you don't come tonight and have a talk with my sister WE ALL MIGHT JUST CHANGE OUR MINDS!!!, bye,' he said as he rushed out the door.

Tyler would never do anything to hurt Jake and hated to say that but he felt he had to for Jake's own good, and Jenna's. 'You know, said Byron on their way back to Millie's, you're pretty smart yourself.' Tyler smiled, that did make him feel a little better.

'There you are said Millie as they entered the bakery. The girls will be ready in ten minutes, she said flustered and you're not even dressed.

'Well I'm not a girl said Tyler, I'll be ready in five, he said as he skipped upstairs.'

'Oh,' gasped Millie as Byron laughed.

Jake still hadn't moved from his front window. He watched as they all got into Byron's limousine and drove off. He couldn't see them really well but they all looked so happy. Jake realised that he was raised by his parents to believe it was his place to watch everyone else have the happy family relationships. And although Millie and Ben were like family and genuinely loved him he knew they also felt sorry for him.

He no longer worried that Jenna would turn him down but did he have what it took to make a relationship work.

What was he doing, he thought, those wonderful people wanted him to be a part of them. But then he thought of his parents who taught him that he was just a big problem, a nuisance, not worth dealing with. Although Ben and Millie tried to teach him differently, his first years spent with his parents scarred him deeply. But Byrons words kept ringing over and over in his head, "it's what you didn't do, Jake and it hurt her deeply". The last thing Jake would ever want to do is hurt Jenna. In fact his avoidance of her was only to make her happy as he believed he wasn't good enough for her or any one, as his parents had taught, but maybe he was going about this all wrong.

He knew about Byron's job at the hospital as a psychiatrist, helping people figure out their lives, and thought perhaps he was right. It was worth a try to make Jenna happy. Jake also thought Tyler had a good point, Tyler was never afraid to speak his mind, Jake thought that maybe tonight he should be more like him.


He went upstairs and got dressed. He opened his drawer to get some clothes and saw the only thing he had left of his parents, a picture of them on their wedding day. They were dressed in their Sunday best, married at the court house in the town where his mother was from. Jake recalled how they had ruined their own lives and decided he wouldn't let them ruin his life any longer.

He picked up their picture, ripped it in two tossed it in the trash.

Just doing that gave him a strong sense of freedom and empowerment he never knew before. Jakes spirits lifted more and more as he got ready for the ball. He looked at the trash can and wished he had done that a long time ago but then he thought it seemed cruel to toss them out like garbage, like something his father would do so he picked up the torn pieces, but he didn't want to put them back in his drawer, he was wondering what to do with it when suddenly he heard a loud bang, then another, he looked out the window and saw firework light the sky.

Richville and Midville decided that they would honour Pleasantville by donating the fireworks they would have used had they won. It was a spectacular display, though they only set a few as a way of gathering everyone, and saved the rest for later. Jake forgot what he was holding in his hand, hurriedly shoved it in his pocket, like a crumpled up piece of paper, and rushed out the door.

As he left his house, dressed in his new suit, he had bought on the trip to the mainland, Jake felt like a new man. The town seemed deserted; he knew the party started about an hour ago. Ben had wanted to leave to go and get him but Byron and Millie both said to let Jake come on his own time. Jake walked quickly to the hall, anxious to see everyone he loved so much, especially Jenna.
He came around the Christmas tree so fast that he knocked into someone. He looked to see Jenna standing there.
'Where's the fire?!?!?' she asked a little annoyed, mostly because she had given up and left the party, thinking Jake would never come. But she didn't realise who she had bumped into. They both stepped back. 'Jake??? Is that, really you???' Jenna realised that she had never seen Jake all dressed up.
'Jenna??? You look . . . I mean, wow. This new Jake found that he could really speak his mind. You look amazing.' Jenna was a little stunned, and not just because she banged into him. She didn't expect those words to come out of his mouth, but she wasn't going to let that stop her.
'You finally noticed me said Jenna and all it took was a five hundred dollar dress!'
'It's not the dress said Jake, I mean it's nice, but . . . Jenna was shocked as Jake put his hands on her shoulders. Jenna, I've always noticed you, always. And I always put you so high above me that I couldn't reach you.' Jenna felt like she'd lost her breath for a moment.
'I never wanted to be above you Jake.'
'I know, he replied but I Just wanted what was best for you and I just didn't think I was it.'

Jenna felt her heart melting fast, she had never stood this close to him, but she was still a bit annoyed, she took a step back.

'Alright said Jenna, who are you and what have you done with the real Jake.'

Jake smiled, she had seen him smile before but never like this, this one was different, this one made her feel . . . well she couldn't describe it but she knew she had never felt like this before. Jake stepped back and took her hands sending shock waves to her heart.

'Jenna, there are so many things I want to tell you, Iv'e wanted to tell you for years, but . . . Jake realised Jenna was on her way somewhere when he nearly ran her over. Were you going somewhere?'

'Huh, said Jenna lost in his eyes, oh, yes I was going home to start packing' she said deciding to be truthful more to see his reaction than anything else. This new Jake was really interesting.

'Are you planning a trip' he asked?

'No she answered, planning on leaving, to the mainland.'

Jakes heart crushed a little on hearing that. 'Actually, he said I was planning on doing the same thing myself.'

'Really, said Jenna, sceptical, why.'

'To get away from . . . from, someone.

'The snob sisters' asked Jenna?

'No, someone else, someone important to me, because I could no longer look into her beautiful face, or listen to her beautiful laugh or the softness of her beautiful voice. It drove me insane because I was too afraid to tell her how I really felt, but not anymore. How about you' he asked releasing her hands.

'Huh?' She replied embarrassed that she was lost in him again.

'Why where you leaving' he asked?

Jenna thought about his description of the beautiful face, laugh, and soft voice and felt it fit her description of him perfectly.

'Pretty much the same' same reason she said.

Jake, paused, smiled, oh that smile again, she thought to herself, will I survive this, then he took another step closer to her and put a hand on her shoulder, 'Jenna I'm sorry if I caused you any pain, but it was only because I, . . . he raised his hand to her cheek and sighed, I care about you, so deeply, (and she didn't know how she was still standing) I thought I was doing the right thing but I was such an idiot, Jenna, please don't go, if you think you can forgive me, please stay, and give me a chance to make it all up to you. I swear I'll spend the rest of my life making it up to you.'

Jenna couldn't believe her ears or stop the tears from raining down her face, and she certainly couldn't find her voice in that unforgettable moment, she stepped into him and with slight hesitation he remembered the old Jake, timid and unsure, but he gently wrapped his arms around her and held her close as the old Jake melted away along with Jenna's heart.

'Listen Jenna I'm always gonna believe you'd be better off with someone else, she shook her head no, Jenna, your amazing, but I'm willing to give this a chance if you are.'

He wiped her tears away, she looked up into his face and noticed his eyes tearing a little too.'

She smiled and nodded yes and hugged him tightly.

The mice who were silently listening from the Christmas tree all cheered loudly and made Jenna jump.

Gregory gave Jake a hi five and a wink to Jenna.

Luckily there was no one else around at the moment, but people started coming out of the hall to rest on the benches under the lights. They had been dancing inside.

'Would you like to dance' asked Jake?

'Yes I would, replied Jenna but I didn't know you danced.'
'I don't know either said Jake but now's a good time to find out.'
'Alright' said Jenna as she laughed and took his hand.

As they entered the hall cheers rang out for them. Jenna wasn't expecting that and felt a little embarrassed but Jake ignored it and led her out on to the dance floor.
Tyler yelled, 'way to go Jake'. Everyone laughed, while Jenna turned a darker red.
After the song was finished, Jake led Jenna to seat by Millie and then walked over to the podium.
'Hello everyone, are you having a good time, he said in a cheery confident voice so unbecoming. Ben and Millie looked at Jenna, who shrugged and smiled. We're so glad you came eventhough this hall is a little small, I promise you a bigger one next year. I know there are many of you who like to dance and many of you who like to be under the lights and now as I flick this switch you can do both.'
The people outside were surprised to hear the music but were glad and started dancing. Others joined them from inside, it was fun dancing outside under the stars in the warm glow of the tree lights.

Jake noticed Charlie and his boys in the corner, 'Hey Charlie, why don't you and your boys help move some of these tables outside so everyone can sit out there?'
'Why don't you move them yourself yelled Charlie' who was jealous of all the attention Jake was getting. Jake hopped over the podium and landed on the floor and headed straight for Charlie. Everyone froze, especially Charlie but he quickly came to his senses before Jake reached him, he certainly didn't look like a push over this time. 'You heard the guy, he yelled to his mates; let's get these tables outta here.'

Jake smiled as he picked up one end of a table that Charlie had. Others joined in and helped out. Ben, Millie, Jenna and Tyler all stood there with there mouths hung opened.

'Hey Jake, said Charlie you wanna join our gang?'

'No thanks, replied Jake, I never liked your gang, besides Iv'e got my own gang thanks.' He walked over to Jenna and her family, leaving Charlie and his crew with their mouths hung opened.

There was such confidence in his step. Jenna was seeing him in a different light and she really liked what she saw.

Everyone was impressed with him but she thought he was ... amazing.


After a few dances Jake and Jenna found a secluded bench under one of the brightly lit trees, and watched as other couples danced by. Ben and Millie being one of the couples were having a wonderful time together.

Matt and Tyler were having a great time too because Billy was able to come, his treatments were working and he was allowed to come home for Christmas. When Billy and his family returned home that night they would find a stack of presents left on their doorstep from many different people, including Byron and Cynthia.


'You seem unusually quiet tonight,' noticed Jake is everything ok?

Huh said Jenna, oh, yea, everything is perfect, actually more than perfect. It's almost like the last twenty years never happened and we never grew apart. What happened to us Jake? We used to sit in these trees she said looking up, we talked about everything, we used to be so close, what happened?'

'We grew up said Jake. Guys were falling all over themselves just to go out with you; I didn't know how to compete with them.'

'Compete? Said Jenna you never had to compete, you only had to ask. Did I ever go out with any of those guys?'

Jake look at all those other guys, where are they now? Not one of them have done as well as you, and you have come so far with so little help. Tonight everyone thinks you're so amazing Jake, but I know you always have been.'

'You're the amazing one Jenna, he said brushing her hair aside, I always thought so. Jenna was speechless again and there was an awkward silent moment.

Do you remember, said Jake back in grade six or seven we studied about time capsules?' Yes said Jenna, it was grade seven, we were twelve.'

'Right said Jake, do you remember that we made our own time capsule and buried it behind your house?'

'Yes laughed Jenna although I don't remember what we put in there.'

'I think we should go dig it up' said Jake.

'Now asked Jenna? We're really not dressed for digging.'

'We didn't bury it that deep he said as he rose and took her hand, common.'

'O.k. said Jenna; I have to admit I'm curious about what's in there.' They headed for Jenna's place.

'What changed you Jake?'

'You he replied, well it was something Byron said about you.'

Jenna gave him a quizzical look.

'He said I hurt you by being so shy and not asking you to the ball, actually Jenna I tried to ask you a few times.

You did???Jenna felt bad.

'But you were always so busy.'

'And grumpy' added Jenna.

'Jake laughed, well I had made up my mind to ask you right after supper that night, the night Byron showed up.'

'Oh no said Jenna, I had no idea.'

'Well it turned out better this way, confessed Jake, but I never meant to hurt you.'

'I know said Jenna, it's the other way around I wanted to hurt you, to make you jealous.'

'Your plan worked very well smiled Jake.' Jenna smiled too. 'And I'm glad it did, it made me realise what I was losing.'

They had arrived at the bakery; there was a shovel out back leaning up against the house.

'Do you remember where the spot is asked Jenna?'

'Yea said Jake, I thought of digging it up many times, just to remember the good days.'

'Why didn't you,' asked Jenna?

Jake looked at her and smiled, 'it just wouldn't be the same without you.'

He dug a hole and didn't have to go too far before he hit something. He brought up an old can and brushed off the dirt. Jenna smiled and was getting excited to find what was in the can. They sat on the chair swing on the back porch and opened the can. Jake pulled out a plastic bag that held their treasures and carefully emptied its contents to reveal a small stuffed teddy, a small doll, a few marbles, a toy truck with no wheels, and some folded up pieces of paper.

I remember this said Jenna as she picked up the teddy; I remember thinking that I was finally old enough to go to sleep without it. As Jake looked at his old toys he wished he had left the can buried. The truck had no wheels when it was given to him at Christmas, but he loved it, and the marbles he had found in the playground. These were his prized possessions but he gave them up for their time capsule.

Jake never stopped to think that sharing this moment with Jenna, of something they did together would bring back deep sorrow from the past, but he didn't say anything.

He carefully opened a folded piece of paper, it was a picture Jenna drew of her family, he smiled and handed it to her.

'Oh my' she said fighting back tears.

'Maybe this wasn't a good idea' said Jake, knowing how she missed her parents.

'I think it's a perfect idea said Jenna with a sniff. She opened the other piece of paper and saw Jakes drawing of a house. This is very good Jake' she said passing it to him. He saw the picture he drew of a house he thought he would like to live in some day.

'It looks like something an architect would draw said Jenna, not a grade seven student. Jake smiled, 'what should we do with it he asked?'

'I want to keep the pictures' said Jenna.

'I want to put this back said Jake as he picked up the truck and the marbles to toss in the bag, but when he picked up the bag he noticed a little box in the bottom of it that stayed behind.

'I don't remember this' he said as he set his toys down and pulled out the box.

Jenna gasped.

'What is it asked Jake?'

'It's . . . for you,' she replied.

Jake opened the box to reveal a bracelet made of string and beads.

'Made that in our grade nine arts class,' said Jenna.

Jake smiled as he held up the bracelet and then he noticed another folded piece of paper. He put the bracelet down and opened the folded paper to see something which really made this all of this worth it, worth a look into the past.

Written on the page were the words I LOVE YOU JAKE and then there was a heart and it was signed by Jenna.

'I couldn't hold it in any longer said Jenna so I wrote it down, dug up our treasure, and buried this with the rest of it. Then I tried to forget about it, about you and how

I felt about you. I even tried dating a few guys in college, and you know what the funny thing is? These guys were from Richville, and they still couldn't measure up to you, so I gave up on dating and threw myself into my studies, I figured a career would take my mind off you because it would take up all my time, but that didn't work either. That's why I decided to leave, I never thought this day would come, she took a deep breath, when I could tell you, her eyes started to water, Jake, I love you.'

Jake embraced her and held her tight as the tears ran down her face.

'I love you too Jenna, with all my heart, it's not much but it's all yours.'

Jenna sighed, 'it's the biggest heart I've ever seen' she said. She looked up into his face, he brushed a tear and without thinking he kissed her, it was greater than he ever imagined. This wasn't so hard, he was glad he didn't stop to think about it or he might have lost his nerve. Not only had he found love, but he had found himself, through Jenna.

Byron was right, Jenna could show Jake a lot of things about himself, and he was eager to learn.

'This is the best night of my life Jenna, thanks to you.'

'Mine too said Jenna, but it was you who started it all, turned my life around.'

Jake smiled looked down at their treasures.

'Should we bury it again asked Jenna?

'Well I'm going to wear this forever' said Jake as he held up the beaded bracelet.

Jenna helped him fasten it around his wrist. He picked up the little box with Jenna's love note. And put it in his inside pocket next to his heart, 'I'm keeping that too' he said. Then he remembered the picture of his parents.

'There is something I would like to bury though.' He pulled out the torn pieces of his parents wedding picture.

'I was going to throw this out but it didn't feel right, they did give me life, if nothing else.'

'And without you said Jenna I would never find happiness, but perhaps it is time to bury the past.'

'Once and for all,' added Jake. He didn't think that the picture would preserve very well in there but he didn't care, he laid the pieces inside, along with his marbles and broken truck and Jenna's doll and teddy.

Jake layed the can back in the hole and piled the dirt back in while Jenna sat their art work on a table just inside the door.

The fireworks started up again.

'We should get back' said Jake.

'We will but first I just want to make sure that this best night of my life isn't just a dream.'

Jake smiled, 'how do we do that,' he asked?

'Like this,' said Jenna as she kissed him. Jake never knew he could feel so incredible.

'Works for me' he said. Jenna laughed. 'Common she said. I feel like a dance.'

What a spectacular night it was, one that would live on in their memories forever. The entire island and the Mainland would talk about this night for years and years. Ben and Millie were so happy for Jake and Jenna and so were many others.

And the mice, the dear wonderful sweet mice, loved their new home and thought that the fireworks were the biggest most incredible trees they had ever seen. They just didn't understand why they were so noisy and didn't stay lit up. Gregory would remember to ask Ben about that later when he got a chance.

After a few dances Jake and Jenna walked into the hall where they saw Cynthia and Byron, Cynthia's parents and Millie and Ben at a table enjoying the refrements.

'Come join us' said Millie as Byron pulled up a couple more chairs. 'Are you haveing a good time' asked Millie?

'Fabulous' said Jenna

'Well I think all that's about to change said Byron, here comes mother.' Byron's mother approached their table along with another man.

'Well done, said Mrs Edwards with a smile, Merry Christmas everyone and congratulations.' 'Thank you' said Ben.

'So we have a wedding to plan and this is Anthony Peters the best wedding planner in the entire mainland.'

'Mother!!! said Byron, we don't have to start right away, it's Christmas.'

'Of course said Mrs Edwards but there's so much to consider and he's just going to give us a few ideas to think about over the holidays.'

'But it's not up to him mother or even you.'

'I know, of course, your right but I just want to help.'

'No mother what you want is to make our wedding the social event of the year. Richville didn't win the Christmas contest; perhaps we can win the wedding contest? We just want a simple wedding, probably in Midville, and it's up to Cynthia and her mother to decide the details.' Byron seemed to be taking a page out of Jakes book; he certainly decided not to be ruled by his mother any longer and his mother seemed to know her place as she looked both shocked and defeated.

'I can do simple said Anthony, I have done simple and made it look elegant.'

'Perhaps, said Mrs Norris, a wedding planner isn't such a bad idea, I'm sure we could use a little help.'

Mrs Edwards beamed at her. 'And since I brought him I will cover all the charges she said.'

'As long as Cynthia and her mom approve of everything' warned Byron.

'Absolutely,' said Mrs Edwards.

At that Byron, Jake, and Ben got up. Jenna looked at Jake but Cynthia grabbed her hand for support, everyone seemed to know more about her wedding than she did.

'You girls plan a wedding said Jake, we won't be far.'

Ben went to check on the mice and Jake and Byron sat on a bench just outside the door, Byron wanted to be in ear shot of his mother. 'So how is everything going' he asked Jake? Jake's smile answered it all.

'You were right Byron, in the last hour I danced with her, kissed her and confessed my love, as did she, and it's all thanks to you.'

'You did it all, said Byron, you just needed a little encouragement.'

'Your little encouragement has changed my life' said Jake.

'No said Byron you changed your life, you always had it in you. You actually gave me hope.' 'How's that' asked Jake?

'I have counselled a lot of troubled people said Byron and not many have made the great leap you have made, and all in one night.'

'You must have done something right said Jake with a laugh. There's one more thing I'd like you to do.'

'Sure said Byron, what?'

'Christmas is the day after tomorrow and Id like to surprise Jenna with a ring, I know it's kind of fast.'

Byron laughed 'I'm sure Jenna will feel she's waited long enough.'

'Yea said Jake, your right, I was wondering if you could tell me where to find one.'

'I know just the place said Byron and I even know just the ring.'

'You do?'

'Yes sir said Byron, when Jenna and I when to Crystal Palace Jewellers to pick out a ring for Cynthia, we decided to separate and see what we could find and then compare. We each ended up with the same ring. She fell in love with it.'

'I have to get that ring' said Jake.

'You will, said Byron, first thing tomorrow. You tell everyone I need help with a present I'm building for Cynthia because she likes home made things, and meet me at my place at ten.'

'Your place at ten said Jenna, startling them, what for.'

'Oh Jakes going to help me build a present for Cynthia' said Byron.

'She likes homemade things' added Jake.

'And I forgot till tonight, you won't tell her will you' asked Byron?

'Course not said Jenna, perhaps I could help.' The guys looked at eachother, they weren't expecting this.

'Yes said Byron you could keep her busy.'

'I want to do some shopping on the mainland tomorrow said Jenna, last minute Christmas shopping, I'll bring her with me and we'll meet for supper at the bakery.'

'Sounds like a plan' said Byron, sometimes you can be so devious.

'I know' said Jenna with a sly smile.

'How's the wedding planning going' asked Byron? Jenna smiled. 'That bad is it, Mother ruling the show?'

'Actually, it's not that bad, said Jenna, your mother has . . . really changed, and her wedding planner does have some really good ideas.'

Byron peeked around the corner to see Cynthia laughing. 'Cynthia seems to be enjoying herself' he said.

'She is said Jenna, she just wanted me to make sure you boys didn't feel deserted.'
'Not at all' said Byron.
'We understand' said Jake.
'Good said Jenna, well I better get back, we shouldn't be too much longer.'
'We'll be here' said Jake with a smile.

Before too long the wedding party broke up with everyone quite pleased about the decisions that were made. Mrs Edwards was so thrilled about the way things were going that she even offered to take Cynthia shopping for a wedding gown at a very expensive wedding boutique. Cynthia was stunned but her mother stepped in and said 'that won't be necessary Cynthia already has a wedding gown, it belonged to my grandmother and is tradition that every girl in the family wears it. My mother wore it and I wore it.' Now Mrs Edwards was stunned but quickly piped up, 'I'm sure it will be just perfect.'
'Cynthia was relieved, although she didn't really believe Mrs. Edwards' last remark, but she didn't really want to wear that old wedding gown either.

Jenna was glad to get back to Jakes side; she was afraid it was all a dream till he put his arm around her and made her heart all a flutter. Every one danced a bit more before the crowd dispersed for home.
Jake walked Jenna home, they took their time though enjoying the lingering moments of a magical night.
'Tonight was wonderful said Jenna looking at Jakes hand clasped in hers. I can hardly believe you're holding my hand and that we danced and . . . kissed but it was well worth the wait.'
'I'm glad you think so said Jake as he took her face in his hands and kissed her right there on the sidewalk. When

they opened their eyes they noticed a few snowflakes fall between them. 'But you don't have to wait any longer,' he said as he kissed her again.

'Jake, people are . . . staring.'

'Are they said Jake smiling into her eyes? All I can see is you Jenna, she smiled. After they got to her house he gave her one last long kiss to dream on. I'll see you in the morning he said.'

'I can't wait,' she answered as she went inside. Ben and Millie were having a warm cup of cocoa at the table in the corner window.

'Hello dear,' said Millie almost startling Jenna, look at the snow, I always love a hot cup of cocoa on the first snowfall, come join us, she said as she poured a cup for Jenna.

'Ok' replied Jenna as she sat and sipped some cocoa. 'Are you happy' asked Ben?

'Very much so, replied Jenna it's been an incredible night.'

'Incredible? Tonight was nothing short of a miracle said Millie, nothing short of a miracle.

# Chapter Eighteen

## Happy Christmas

The next morning after breakfast Jake and Jenna drove to Cynthia's house. After a nice kiss goodbye, Jenna hopped out and Jake carried on to Byron's. Byron was just coming out of the door and he noticed a pile of wood in the back of Jakes truck. 'What's with all the wood he asked, are you making a delivery on Christmas Eve?'

'Sure am, said Jake, right here.'

'What said Byron I don't think dad ordered it.'

'No, replied Jake, you did.'

'I did' asked Byron?

'Well I brought this wood for two reasons, said Jake, first because I had to make it look to Jenna like you were really building something and second because I realised last night that I can't lie to Jenna, I couldn't sleep till I decided that you are actually going to build Cynthia a hutch for your new home.

'Oh am I' said Byron surprised, I don't know anything about carpentry.'

'Got everything you need right here and I'll help you said Jake, besides Jenna will probably be asking about it when she gets back and I won't have to make another lie.'

'You're a good man said Byron with a smile, Jenna's a lucky girl, and actually I think this is a really good idea Jake.'

'Yea?'

'Yes, studies have shown that the majority of women like home made things from their mate some even prefer them, it has a more sentimental meaning to them.'

'Really said Jake?'

'Yes said Byron, you really underestimate your talent, I bet Cynthia will love this so much that you'll probably have to help me build her something every year.' Jake laughed, 'sure thing' he said.

'But first we have a ring to buy' said Byron, as he walked to his car.

'Right said Jake as he followed, so, did Cynthia agree to go shopping with Jenna.'

'Absolutely answered Byron and she promised to keep her busy till supper time.'

'Great said Jake, how did you get her to do that, Jenna was worried about how to keep Cynthia busy all day.'

'Oh, well, said Byron, that was simple, I told her the truth, I told her we would be looking for a ring for Jenna and since we didn't have her to help us it would probably take all day. She's so, so, thrilled and excited for Jenna and you, but she's promised to keep it secret.'

'That's good' smiled Jake.

Byron pulled up in front of the store. Jake noticed all the traffic, 'it looks busy' he said.

'They always have a big Christmas Eve sale said Byron, but don't worry I called the jeweller this morning and explained the ring we wanted and he said he'd have it ready.'

'Oh good' said Jake as they entered.

As Jake looked around he thought heaven must look something like this, everything sparkled from ceiling to floor. They walked up to the front counter where some other people were also looking at rings.

'Ah yes Mr Byron Edwards said an attendant I will get the ring you requested.'

He was back in a flash with a box but when he opened it the box was empty Jake and Byron looked at the empty box then at eachother then to the attendant. He wondered what their puzzled looks were about till he too looked in the box.

'OHH the attendant gasped, MARTIN!!!' he yelled, but he didn't have to, Martin was only a few feet away serving another man.

'Yes,' Martin answered?

'Where is the ring that was in this box, demanded the attendant!!!!?'

'Oh you mean this one said Martin holding up the ring?'

'Hey said Byron that's the ring.'

'But he offered to pay twenty five hundred, five hundred more than the asking price.'

'I'll pay three thousand' said Jake.

The attendants and the other man looked at him in surprise. That's when Jake noticed how well dressed everyone was, dressed as though they were going to church, even Byron looked as though he might be dressed for the office. It never dawned on Jake you'd have to dress up to go shopping, he was after all going to be spending most of the day working, and he did after all put on his best plaid shirt. He was surprised that the attendants looked as though they didn't believe him, but Byron nodded in Jake's defence and they immediately accepted it.

'I'll pay thirty five hundred' said the other man.

'Four thousand' said Jake quickly. Again the attendants looked to Byron for approval.

'You don't know who this is' said Byron a little annoyed. This is Jake Anderson, the famous carpenter from Pleasantville, winner of the Christmas tree contest.'

'Jake's tool barn' asked the other customer?'

Jake nodded nervously because he honestly couldn't remember ever seeing the man.

'You're the one who donated all the materials and your time to restore the Midville nursing home?'

'Yea,' said Jake still feeling unsure about all of this.

'Well I can't thank you enough said the man as he grabbed Jakes hand to shake it. If you hadn't been so generous my mother in law would have had to move in with us.'

'Oh,' laughed Jake.

'Yea and it's no laughing matter said the man. So here, he said placing the ring in Jakes' hand; you've earned this and my deepest gratitude for the rest of my life.'

'Thank you' said Jake.

'Don't mention it said the man, please.'

Martin took the man to another counter to look at more rings.

'I told you said Byron, you under estimate your own talent.'

Jake smiled 'so he said to the attendant we'll take this ring.'

'At the original price' added Byron.

'Of course,' said the attendant, feeling like he had just lost a couple thousand dollars, but since Byron's family were big customers he dared not complain.

'And I'll take this too' said Jake pointing to a beautiful gift set of earings and a necklace to match.

'This is six hundred dollars' said the attendant laying it on the counter. 'And I want this too' said Jake pointing to a set of gold bracelets.

'These are two hundred and fifty dollars apiece, do you want all three?'

'Yes, smiled Jake, I don't think Jenna has anything like this he said taking out his wallet, and she deserves it all.' 'That's quite a bit' said Byron.

'It comes to two thousand, eight hundred and ninety five dollars, with tax' said attendant doubtful.

'I know it sounds like a lot said Jake, counting out his money, but I have a lot to make up for; I didn't build Jenna anything homemade and I don't know if this is gonna do it.'

The attendant looked shocked to think that something homemade could out do his fine jewels. Byron bursted out laughing and couldn't stop. The complex look on both Jake and the jeweller's faces made him laugh even that much harder. But the jeweller was smiling as he finished counting Jakes money.

'If you will wait just a minute he said I will gift wrap each of them for you.'

'O.k., thanks' said Jake. The jeweller was back in a few short minutes with four beautifully wrapped boxes. 'Here is the diamond ring, he said as he laid it on the counter, and the necklace set, the bracelets and for making me the biggest seller of the day another fine gold necklace on the house.'

'Thanks said Jake, Jenna's gonna think she died and went to heaven. Merry Christmas he said as he shook the attendants hand vigorously.'

'Thank you said the attendant, surprised and a very merry Christmas to you too.' The attendant handed Jake a bag with his gifts in it.

The rest of the day was spent at Byron's place building Cynthia's hutch. Even the Mayor pitched in and decided that maybe next year the guys would get together and have a day for building Christmas presents for their wives and perhaps they could go one step further and make toys for needy children. Jake thought it was a great idea and he would save scrap wood throughout the year. Byron thought some of his patients would benefit from helping out and he was right.

Santa's workshop would be built next to the hospital and bring joy to many underprivileged families, both on the island and the main land. Mayor Edwards even found money in the budget to provide employment at the Santa's workshop in Richville and also the one Jake would build in Pleasantville on the piece of land across from the tool barn, where his old house once stood. He didn't know what to do with it before but this, he thought was perfect.

Around three o'clock the hutch was finished and Byron was quite pleased and impressed with it. 'Cynthia will never believe I made this' he said.

'But you did said Jake, I just gave you a few pointers.'

'Yea I guess' said Byron.

'You under estimate your own talent said Jake with a smile.' Byron laughed.

As Jake drove home he was pretty pleased with the way things turned out. When he arrived at his place he noticed some boxes of supplies he had ordered but he hadn't unpacked yet, so he thought he would take a look, while he had a couple hours. He noticed as he opened the first one that lying right on the top was the answer he was looking for. Even after everything he had bought Jenna it still bothered him that he didn't have anything homemade to give her for Christmas especially after what Byron said about women liking homemade things so much. But he didn't know what to do till now.

Companies would often send along a free promotional tool, something new in case Jake might be interested in selling them and he often was. This time instead of sending a tool they sent a few wooden craft kits with all the pieces all ready cut out, you just have to put them together. It was a new idea, it wouldn't be totally homemade but it would be something Jake put together for Jenna and it wouldn't take very long. He could engrave her name on the top of it to give it that homemade feel. It was perfect and Jake would definitely order more kits of every kind, most of which were toys, he thought they would be a great idea for Santa's workshop, especially for those who weren't really handy with tools.

By six o'clock everyone had arrived at the bakery. Jake had gotten there first and put the wrapped up jewellery box under the tree in the living room along with his presents for Ben, Millie and Tyler. The rest of Jenna's presents he gave to Ben, to hide for him. But the ring he kept with him.

Byron picked up the girls at the ferry landing and headed for the Bakery. Jenna had her arms loaded with parcels when Jake met her at the door. 'Can I help you' he asked? 'NO she answered hastily, I mean, Cynthia's helping and um, we'll be right down' she said as she rushed up the stairs to her room, with Cynthia right behind her.
'That was close,' Jenna said as they lay the presents on her bed. 'I know, said Cynthia but I don't think he saw anything.'

While they were shopping Jenna had seen a nice display of men's clothes and she knew that 99%of Jakes wardrobe consisted of work clothes, plaid shirts, and jeans. These new clothes looked casual enough for Jake to wear, but still dressy enough to go out in. Jenna realised that Jake would never buy these on his own because he wasn't much of a shopper. Cynthia also thought it was an excellent idea, luckily Jake and Byron were the same size and Cynthia knew the right size. So Jenna bought several nice shirts, sweaters and pants and a really nice Jacket.

They hurried back down stairs to enjoy the wonderful meal that Millie and Ben had put on. It was a wonderful evening and although the festivities of the past few days were amazing, everyone seemed to enjoy this time together most of all.

Jenna was up late wrapping presents, she had to show Millie the gifts she had bought for Jake. Millie thought it was a perfect idea and that the clothes were lovely, she had the same idea for Ben. When Jenna later put the presents under the tree she saw her present there from Jake and smiled.

By seven o'clock Christmas morning Tyler was hollering for everyone to get up. He just couldn't wait any longer. He had even waken the mice and called Jake to come over. Jake brought the bike that Ben had bought for Tyler and hid it in the kitchen. Everyone gathered around the tree, including the mice. Millie said a prayer of thanks and everyone started opening presents. Millie loved her new coat she got from Ben along with a beautiful sweetheart necklace. Ben liked his new clothes, and the nice new watch Millie had given him. Jake was surprised when he saw all the nice new clothes he got from Jenna, he wasn't expecting that, but he was glad to have them and he really loved the Jacket. He even picked out, in his mind the suit of clothes he would wear the next time he went shopping at Crystal Palace Jewellers, he was never going there in work clothes ever again. 'Wow I'm really glad to have these' he said to Jenna.
'Do you really like them' she asked?
'Like them, he replied I've never had clothes so nice.' He gave her a hug and a kiss. Tyler loved the new toys he got from everyone and was glad he didn't get clothes; he couldn't understand what all that fussing was about.
'Hey Ben, said Jake, I think you forgot something in the kitchen.' As Ben went out to the kitchen Jenna opened her gift from Jake. 'Oh it's lovely she said looking at the jewellery box with her name on it. I've never had anything with my name on it, thank you, I love it.' Jenna didn't want to tell Jake she had nothing to put in it.
Just then everyone jumped as Tyler yelled 'AHHHH!!!!' The mice all scurried up the Christmas tree which made it rattle and a ball or two fell off. 'Uncle Ben!' It was all Tyler could say as he hopped on his new bike to get the feel of it. It had

a wire basket attached to the front of it and there were some parcels in it.

'It's time to make your first delivery' Ben said as he pointed to Jenna. Tyler happily waddled his bike over to Jenna. 'I guess these are for you he said as he looked at the tags, Looks like they're all from Jake.' Jenna smiled as she took the first box and opened it to reveal the necklace and earring set. Jenna almost lost her breath.

'OH, oh Jake.'

'Do you like it' he asked?

'It's stunning, it's too much.'

'It's not enough, said Jake luckily there's more.' Jenna's hands were shakeing as she picked up the next box, this one had the bracelets. 'Oh my, they're beautiful. Jake you really shouldn't have.'

'Yes I should have, a long time ago. He handed her the last box. It had the chain necklace he had gotten for free from the grateful jeweller, so Jake had bought a gold heart charm with the letter J engraved in the center of it. J for Jenna' he said.

'No said Jenna. J for Jake and you'll always be the center of my heart.' She picked it up and fastened it around her neck. She took a deep breath of relief grateful that there were no more boxes to open. Now I have something to put in my jewellery box' she said as she leaned forward to hug him, but stopped dead as she saw Jake holding a little purple velvet box. Her heart jumped to her throat. Millie started crying.

'I'll open this one for you,' he said. Jenna's jaw dropped when she saw the ring that was sitting in the box.

'Byron helped me pick it out, Jenna; he said as he got down on one knee, this is something else I should have done a long time ago. Jenna couldn't stop the tears so Jake thought he had better hurry. I love you Jenna, I have always loved you, I've just been too . . .' Jenna put her hand on his lips; she couldn't bear the thought of him saying something bad about himself. He took her hand and kissed it. Will you marry me? With a happy 'yes' she threw herself into his arms and kissed him. Jake slipped the ring on her finger. Millie rushed over to see, wiping her tears.

'Oh Millie look, it's the one I fell in love with. Oh Jake it's perfect, thank you so much for everything, I love it and I love you.'

Jake had such a great feeling inside him for finally making Jenna as happy as he thought she always should be.

Later that day, Byron and Cynthia dropped in for a visit and everyone laughed as Byron told them how he and Jake planned their Christmas surprises while the girls were making their wedding plans at the Christmas ball. He also told them how he had to make Cynthia a hutch because Jake couldn't stand lying to Jenna, and about the events that took place at the jewellery store. It made Jenna love Jake all that much more, and Cynthia added that she did want something homemade every Christmas but it didn't have to be as big as the hutch, which she absolutely loved.

'So, said Millie, have you two decided when the big day is? Well, said Cynthia Byron decided he wanted to start the year off right so we're getting married on New Year's Day.'

'In five days, asked Jenna startled, you don't give a girl much notice???!'

'Yup said Byron with a big smile and that girl is Mother, it will keep her from having too much time to get carried away.'

'I think it's a great idea said Cynthia though Lydia was not too pleased.' 'Yea added Byron but when she realised that it was going to be the first wedding of the new year she started coming around and you can bet she's moving heaven and earth to make it the one that all the rest will have to live up to, in the little time she has.

'You'll be my maid of honor Cynthia asked Jenna?' 'Of course said Jenna I'd be honoured.' 'Hope you don't mind Lydia is picking out a dress for you,' Cynthia added.

'I'm sure it will be exquisite smiled Jenna, and you'll be my maid of honour she asked and you can wear any dress you like.' 'Sure said Cynthia, have you decided when.' Jenna looked at Jaked who shrugged, 'hmm she said, I think Valentine's Day would be nice.'

'Ah that's sweet said Cynthia.' 'That's perfect said Millie it will give us time to do lots of baking.' 'What do you think Jake,' asked Jenna?

'That sounds good to me' he answered.

'Oh this is wonderful' said Cynthia.

'Yes it is said Jenna, and I can't wait to see your wedding dress.'

'Well, it's undergoing a few changes, said Cynthia. I really wanted a new one and so did Lydia of course but it meant so much to mom for me to wear the same one she did, thank goodness it doesn't fit and needs a few alterations, so we're going to be using the same material but make it look more modern, Lydia and I looked trough some bridal magazines today and chose a design, she and I both love it and mom's happy with it too.'

'Wow said Jenna, you've been really busy. Yes well we only have five d . . . ahhh!!!!'

'What,' jumped Jenna. 'What is it' said Byron?

A, a, mouse, I thought I saw a mouse under the tree . . . with trousers?'

'Oh said Jenna, Ben collects toy mice from all over the world, through mail order and some of them look very real and are quite fast, we even had some in the town Christmas tree.'

Jenna's family breathed a sigh of relief and we're so grateful that Jenna was such a quick thinker. 'Wow said Byron I'd like to see your mouse collection someday.'
'Well said Ben with a smile and a twinkle in his eye, someday, I think that could be arranged.'

## THE END